the first kiss hypothesis

the first kiss hypothesis

CHRISTINA MANDELSKI

Copyright © 2017 by Christina Mandelski. All rights reserved, including the right to reproduce, distribute, or transmit in any form or by any means. For information regarding subsidiary rights, please contact the Publisher.

Entangled Publishing, LLC
2614 South Timberline Road
Suite 109
Fort Collins, CO 80525
Visit our website at www.entangledpublishing.com.

Crush is an imprint of Entangled Publishing, LLC.

Edited by Heather Howland
Cover design by April Martinez
Cover art from iStock

Manufactured in the United States of America

First Edition November 2017

*To my parents, Richard and Carman Durr, whose love story
is still going strong.
Happy Golden Anniversary
May 11, 2018*

Science tells you love
Is just a chemical reaction in the brain
Let me be your Bunsen burner baby
Let me be your naked flame.

—John Otway

Chapter One

NORA

Today is the annual *Keep Florida Wild!* Ecology Festival, and the air in the Edinburgh High School gym reeks of tofu and onions. Between the Vegan Club's taco stand, a February heat wave, and the broken air conditioner, I admit these aren't ideal conditions to rescue the planet. Or find true love.

But I'm still going to try.

Every year, I've set up my kissing booth and raised money for an endangered animal that gets ignored by mainstream media. Four years in a row, I've had a line of horny high school guys willing to pay for a chance to lock lips with yours truly.

I'm pretty good at raising money. Not so much at finding true love.

My grandmother started me on this path, telling me over and over the story of how she met my grandfather at a kissing booth. He walked up, paid his quarter, they kissed, and ***boom!*** Thunder rumbled, lightning struck, and the earth shook.

They got married two weeks later and were inseparable for forty-three years.

If you hear a story like that enough—and you're obsessed with the laws that govern the universe like I am—eventually you come up with a working scientific theory, a testable hypothesis.

For each person in the world, there is exactly one other person who, at first kiss, causes an immediate and intense reaction.

It's like the chemistry experiment last year when we mixed sugar with sulfuric acid. Instantly, there was smoke and fizz everywhere.

Or, for the nonscientific types out there, true love at first kiss.

And that's why I sit here, charging five bucks a kiss to *SAVE THE GOPHER TORTOISE!*

I glance down the line and sigh. I've kissed a lot of these guys already. That's fine. As long as I'm doing good in the world and there are a few new customers (the kid who just moved here from Texas, and that uber attractive German exchange student), I'm not giving up.

I'm a scientist, after all. I leave no stone unturned.

I'm also prepared, as always. I have germ destroying breath spray. I'll gargle with extra-strength Listerine when it's over. My vaccinations are up to date, so I've minimized the risks. I'm ready to find love in the most sanitary of ways.

Except that next in line is Keaton Drake, so in this case, I know the result.

We kissed at the 80s dance freshman year. Slow dancing to a Madonna song, his hands roaming lower and lower, he gazed at me and our lips touched and...nothing.

He lifts his eyebrows. "Hey, Nora."

Inside, I cringe. I really don't want to kiss him, but it's not like I can pick and choose who gets in line. "Keaton." I nod and reach for the five he's holding.

Think of the gopher tortoises.

"What's with the hair?" he asks.

I fight the urge to smooth it down—it's super curly, which is only made worse by how humid it is in here. Not a good mix. "Just time for a change." Two weeks ago, I found out I was accepted to my dream college. Even if it's a dream that likely won't come true, I wanted to do something big to mark the occasion. Pierce my nose. Get a tattoo. All of which would have given my mother a heart attack. So I decided to let my hair down, after years of wearing it up.

I'm not a huge fan of change, so it feels like a big deal.

Keaton winks. "Pretty sexy."

I hand over the breath spray.

"What's this for?"

"I like to keep things hygienic."

He sprays, and then slowly pushes back his mop of blond hair. He's an athlete, football and baseball, and he thinks he's a sex god.

I lean forward, across the table; he leans in, and his lips touch mine. There's a firmness to this kiss that tells me he's had some experience since he paid his five dollars last year. Just the right amount of moisture. Good for him.

Still, no reaction whatsoever. Not that it matters since, according to my hypothesis, it's only the first kiss that counts.

He smiles. It's not the worst smile. Too bad.

"Thanks, Nor. I hope you save the turtles."

"Tortoises. They're tortoises. Here, take a brochure."

Next is a very skinny freshman. I don't know his name, but his lips are so chapped I almost offer him my lip balm.

He's followed by Paul Betts who kisses like my mouth is a stone wall and his is a battering ram. Every year.

Then Michael Lovejoy, a really good guy who's jaw-droppingly handsome. Too bad kissing him is like kissing my brother, if I had one.

Between customers, I see Abby checking out my booth. We've been friends for a long time, though we don't hang out like we used to. According to what I see online, she's jump-started her social life this year without me. I have no idea how she manages to party while taking five AP classes and making the finals in the state Science Olympiad. She seems to have it figured out, though.

"How's it going over there?" I ask.

"Nora..." She rolls her eyes. "You're going to get the plague."

I shrug. "Anything for science."

She takes a dollar from a kid in exchange for a manatee-shaped cookie. Save the Manatees. Everyone knows about manatees, which is great, but they've got plenty of help. I'm surprised she didn't come up with something more original.

The last bell is about to ring, and my line has fizzled out, just like every kiss. The guy from Texas was a no-show. The exchange student was like a hyper puppy. I kept waiting for him to have an accident on the floor.

Nothing today, but that's okay. I've got time.

"Ms. Reid." Mr. Chaffee, faculty sponsor of the Eco-Fest, stops by my booth, shaking his head. "I believe kissing booths went out of style sometime in the last century." He picks up one of my brochures and smirks. "I get that you want to save the...gopher tortoise? But I can think of at least a dozen noninvasive ways to raise money for a cause."

I smile confidently. After four years, I've thought this through. I point to my handmade sign that clearly states "NO TONGUE." Bold and in all caps, though a few always try to slip through. Hazard of the experiment.

"Well I suppose that's something." He scratches his beard and squints at me. "Really, though. A kissing booth, of all things?"

Also something I've considered. I lift a shoulder. "It's perfect. What hormone-crazed teen is going to say no to a kiss, even if he doesn't care about gopher tortoises? And you never know, maybe one of them will turn out to be a keeper."

His eyes widen. "Oh, so you have an ulterior motive?"

A flash of panic zips through me. "No. NO!" As much as I'd like to share my hypothesis with another scientist, I'm not stupid. He wouldn't get it.

He chuckles. "Good. Because you'd have to kiss a lot of, uh, gopher tortoises, to find a prince in this lot."

My stomach sinks. My hypothesis is controversial, I know. Some might say crazy, which is why I've mostly kept it to myself. I gather up my brochures and glance at him. "The most important thing is, I did just raise a lot of money to save a very adorable reptile species."

"Yeah, you did, I guess. Speaking of..." He pulls a paper out of the folder in his hands and passes it to me. "I printed this out for you. These deadlines are coming up, so if you or your mom need any help, just ask me."

"Thank you, Mr. C." I bite my bottom lip, take the paper, and shove it inside the box with my brochures.

"Anytime," he says and moves on.

Mr. Chaffee is a good guy and a great scientist. He's also my favorite teacher, the one who pushed me toward clinical research, suggested I apply to Emory, and is now giving me scholarship information.

As he moves on to Abby's booth, I wonder about him. He's married with a few little kids, but is he happy? I think about this a lot, about people in general. People meet, go on a date, have that first kiss. Maybe it's an okay kiss, but that's all there is—no fizz, no smoke, no chemical reaction. Maybe that's enough for some people, but I believe that's the universe telling them they're incompatible. That they're inert compounds.

If more people paid attention to that first kiss, the world might be a better place. I've seen what it does, ending up with the wrong person. My parents, for example. Good at first, then boring, then mean, then ugly, and eventually just sad.

Speaking of the wrong person, I look up and lock eyes with Eli Costas, strolling toward me with a slight limp.

Immediately, my brain short-circuits and I forget what I'm doing.

Eli. Neighbor, best friend, part-time chauffeur. That hair, dark and wavy, sticking out in ways that invite you to run your fingers through it. The olive skin like a real-life Greek god, and eyes that look just like the blue oval in the watercolor sets Mom used to buy me when I was little. He's tall, and a lacrosse maniac with an upper body to prove it. Your basic unrealistically attractive high school student usually only found in books or movies. The difference is, he's real, and everyone wants him. Including me. It's a battle I fight daily.

He flashes me a grin. One side of his mouth quirks up higher than the other, and a dimple cuts deep into his cheek. Holy cow.

As he moves into my airspace, I force myself to focus on counting the tortoise money. Five. Ten. Fifteen. Twenty. Twenty-five. Forty. It always takes me a minute or two to get my bearings when it comes to Eli. To remind myself that nothing can happen between us.

It's a sad story. Of all the kissing I've done in the name of science, he was the first. Spring break, eighth grade, Madison Dunn's birthday party. My hypothesis was newly formed, and I had a *huge* crush on him. I was sure that he was the only human I'd ever need to kiss—that he was the lightning, the thunder, the sugar to my sulfuric acid. The night of the party, I decided to prove it.

I followed him into the garage, where he'd gone to get a

Coke from the extra fridge. With total confidence, I kissed him—hard—on those full lips, right there in the glow of the refrigerator light.

It was horrible.

He'd just taken a giant swig of soda, which was probably why his lips were so cold. And then they were just…wet. Zero reaction.

When it was over, he moved in to try again, but I backed away. It was too late.

I shared my hypothesis with him, naively thinking he'd understand. He didn't. He called me crazy, got mad, and wouldn't talk to me. It was terrible. There was nothing I could do, though. I had to trust the result. I believed in my hypothesis. The universe had spoken loud and clear, and Eli became the first failed kiss of my experiment.

Eventually, we made up and went back to being best friends. It should also be noted that my rejection didn't wreck him long term—he's done more than fine with the ladies.

The problem is my crush on him still exists. Not helping is the fact that he's only gotten hotter and funnier and easier to be with.

He sidles up behind me and I catch the slap-you-in-the-face man scent of soap and sweat and Eli. I'm intoxicated by that smell, and have been for a long time.

"I wonder how the gopher tortoises feel, being used like this?" he whispers, close to my ear, so that the little hairs inside stand at attention.

A shiver runs through me and I fumble the pile of cash. "I'm trying to count here?"

He laughs that deep Eli laugh, the one that has always made me feel so safe. I listen for it in the hallways at school. I miss it when we're not together. I love that laugh.

To be completely honest, sometimes I wish we could go back in time to Madison's garage and try again, but the scientist in me knows that's not how it works. My hypothesis is clear: a reaction either happens, or it doesn't.

And as much as Eli tempts me, I will not be one half of an inert compound.

Chapter Two

ELI

Nora seems annoyed, but I don't let that stop me.

I move to her other ear and catch a whiff of the shampoo that she's been using since we were kids. Strawberry passion fruit something or other. "So? Any luck? I didn't sense any seismic activity."

"Shh, I'm counting…"

There's a wad of cash in her hands. Cash she made kissing douchebags like Keaton Drake. She moves her head and her dark copper hair sorta bounces. She's been wearing it down these last few weeks. It looks good.

When I step around her, the scent of strawberries fades and I smell my lacrosse bag. So gnarly. I drop it on the floor. "Just saying. I didn't hear a sonic boom or anything."

She glares at me, like she always does, with those giant brown eyes.

"If you must know"—her steely gaze melts into a disappointed frown—"only the tortoises got lucky this year."

When she stands, my eyes accidentally move over her body. She's wearing tight black jeans and a gray T-shirt that hugs her in the right places. I can't tell her that. We can never be more than friends, she claims. Also, she'd accuse me of objectifying the female body. Which I guess I am.

"You know you're delusional, right?" I ask.

She slides the cash into a yellow envelope. "People thought Thomas Edison was delusional. Electric light? Not possible! Isaac Newton, Marie Curie, Galileo, everyone thought they were nuts." She picks up her book bag. "They were right, though, and so am I. One day I'll prove it and in the meantime, I'm not wasting time with the wrong person."

All the muscles in my body tense up. She means *me*.

This whole bullshit theory comes from Gigi's story about how the first kiss with her future husband supposedly shook the planet off its freaking axis. I know Gigi, though. She didn't mean for Nora to twist it all up into some impossible quest. Nora's just like that dude, Don Quixote, tilting at imaginary windmills. We read that book sophomore year. He was off his rocker, too.

"Okay, Einstein," I say. "You know, theories get proven wrong all the time."

"Yeah, well. Not this one." She slings her bag onto her shoulder. "You ready?"

I grab her box of turtle brochures, accidentally twist funny on the way out the door, and flinch. My bad knee's been bugging me all week, and I should probably do the stretches the physical therapist gave me—

Wait.

Just under the cardboard flap of the box, something catches my attention. It's a printed website page that says EMORY UNIVERSITY SCHOLARSHIPS across the top.

What?

The sun is blazing hot outside the gym. A couple of my

teammates shout from across the parking lot. I wave, but I'm not thinking about them. Nora gets into the truck and I carry the box to the back, then lift the cardboard flap to get a better look at the paper. Emory University, in Atlanta, Georgia. Scholarships. On top of the paper someone's written *Nora, deadlines coming up. Come see me for help!* in red pen.

I stare through the window at the back of her head, at that wild hair.

What the hell is this?

Next year, Nora is going to Citrus State, five miles east of here, with *me.* Her parents don't have much money, and my grades suck, so we both planned to spend the first two years at State. I'll play lacrosse, we'll take our basic courses, then we'll transfer to UF. I'll still play lacrosse, because it's all I'm good at, and eventually figure out something to major in. She'll become a mad scientist and save the world. It's been our plan since freshman year. She has never, *ever* mentioned Emory University.

Why hasn't my best friend told me she applied to a college out of state?

"What's wrong?" she asks when I climb in and yank on my seat belt.

I glare at her. "Nothing."

She flips down the visor mirror and checks her hair. "*Something's* wrong. You look like someone kicked your dog."

More like someone just kicked our friendship to the curb. "I'm fine." I channel all my confusion and anger into making my truck's damn engine turn over, which does not happen.

"Fine," she says. "Just tell me it's a PFE day."

I take a deep breath. PFE is code for "Pie Fixes Everything." Yeah, it's lame as shit, but in our defense, we came up with it when we were nine.

My brain is trying to work out this Emory news and it's

coming up with nothing. "I don't know."

"So no pie?" she says, pleading.

It's a look I've never been very good at resisting.

I try the ignition again, and the third time's a charm. I back out fast, just in case it thinks about dying. "I'm pretty busy, you know. Homework." This is weak. I usually do my homework the period before it's due, if I do it at all. From her silence, I know she's thinking the same thing and wisely decides not to make a smart-ass comment about it.

"Okay, fine. No pie. Homework."

I grumble, unable to ever say no to this girl. "Fine. We can get pie. As long as it's to go."

"You sure you have time? All that homework…"

I glance her way. She's definitely mocking me. I think of that letter in the box. Pie isn't gonna fix this.

"I said we could go, didn't I?"

"Okay. Yes, you did. PFE, *to go.*"

My pulse pumps harder as my truck winds through historic downtown Edinburgh, which is about as exciting as it sounds. Not far from the beach, our town used to be a big tourist destination back in the old days. Now it's rundown as hell. A few antique stores, the funeral home, an old courthouse, a hotel, and the Mermaid diner, which is where we go for pie.

The Mermaid, first of all, sucks. It didn't used to, back when Nora's grandma was their baker. Now Gigi's in an assisted living place and can't remember my name. We still go to the Mermaid, though, because pie is our thing—me and Nora's—and has been since the day we met, the summer before fourth grade.

She and her mom had just moved in with her grandma, Gigi. Nora didn't know anyone, and was sitting on the front porch looking lonely and sad. Mom made me go over. When Nora looked up at me with those big eyes, I didn't know what to say, so I ran into her house and asked Gigi if we could have some pie.

I brought two slices of blueberry out to the porch, and that was it. PFE. By the time the pie was gone, we were laughing at our purple teeth and telling each other everything.

I thought we still did that. The important stuff, anyway. Obviously, I didn't get the memo that we'd stopped.

Donna, the waitress, sets us up with a slice of apple for me and a slice of cherry for Nora, to go. I can tell from the sound of the pie being sliced that it's got a soggy bottom crust. I can hear the apples crunch, which means they aren't cooked through.

Damn, I miss Gigi's pies.

We walk out and get back in the truck. I say nothing, but inside, I'm about to boil over. We had a plan. Is she not even gonna tell me it's off? I tear the wrapper off my plastic fork, open the Styrofoam container, and go after that slice of pie like a hungry lion on an antelope.

She chuckles.

"What's so funny?" I ask.

"I thought you wanted pie *to go*?"

I drop the fork. "This *is* to go. We're gone."

She tilts her head and purses her lips. "You are so predictable."

I know she's talking about how I have zero self-control when it comes to pie, but this comment hits me wrong. *I'm* predictable? That's rich. She's the predictable one with her slice of pie still in the bag on her lap. She's the planner. Scientific. Rational.

Which means she'd never leave her mom and Gigi, I realize.

There's no way she'll go to Emory.

She nudges my arm. "Eli, come on, I'm just messing with you."

I tell myself to relax, feeling the pieces of my life that only Nora holds settle back into place. She's not going anywhere. She'd tell me if she was gonna do something as huge as leaving home.

But that doesn't mean I'm still not pissed she's keeping secrets.

"I know." I turn the key and my engine coughs. Loudly.

"That doesn't sound right."

"Give him a second." I try again. *Cough. Cough.*

She reaches forward, picks at the duct tape that holds the glove box shut. "Maybe it's time to put Michael out of his misery?"

I huff. It's one thing to keep secrets, it's another to insult my truck. "You need to not talk trash about Michael Jordan right now. There's nothing wrong with him."

She shifts in her seat, facing me, and folds her hand in her lap. "You mean besides not being able to start?"

"He'll start, don't worry." Finally, thankfully, he does. "See? And show some respect. If it weren't for this truck, you'd be hitching a ride to school every day, or riding the bus with the freshmen."

A sly smile flickers across her mouth. "If it weren't for me, you wouldn't be making twenty bucks a week doing nothing."

"Oh, I'm doing nothing, am I?"

"Eli." She laughs and it sounds exactly like her nine-year-old self, on Gigi's front porch, pie stains on her teeth. "You don't even have to come and pick me up. I'm *literally* the girl next door."

I can't argue with that, so I don't. We drive in silence down Main until I turn into our neighborhood.

"So…" She breaks the silence. "Any plans this weekend?"

Why even ask? She doesn't give a damn what I do, even if I want her to. "Big party tonight at Koviak's. You wanna come?"

"To a lacrosse party?" She raises an eyebrow as I pull into our driveway and throw MJ into park. "No, thanks."

Surprise, surprise. My anger over the letter and her stupid theory comes to a boil. I bravely stare directly into her eyes— eyes that can make me think things if I'm not careful. "Oh. Right. No new guys to kiss there. Why waste your time?"

She gives me a death glare as she throws open her door, then jumps to the ground.

"Who's predictable now?" I say to her back, and she slams the door closed behind her.

We meet around the back of the truck and I lift out the box, which she yanks from my arms. If she were a cartoon, there'd be smoke coming out of her ears.

I fold my arms across my chest and watch her try to carry all her stuff. "You want some help?"

She stomps off. "No, I do not!"

I can't help watching her cross the driveway, hair wild and blown sideways by the hot breeze. For someone so smart, I can't believe how she clings to this stupid theory.

I grab my lacrosse bag and sling it over my shoulder a little harder than I need to, sending pain searing through my knee. A disturbing thought hits me. The kids who go to State are mostly local, and not the smartest. They let anyone in. Is that what Emory is all about? Maybe she thinks she'll find a better class of guys to kiss up there?

Is that why she didn't tell me? Because she knows I'll call her on that bullshit?

I want to throw something, hard. It's one thing to set up a kissing booth once a year in the high school gym. It's another thing to leave home and everything you know just to prove a messed-up theory.

Anyone with a brain can guess that's not gonna end well. She'll end up sad and alone, except for the cats. She's definitely got cat lady potential.

I walk up our front steps and glance over to her porch, where she's struggling to unlock the door. I have to strangle the urge to go and help her. That's what I do—I help Nora.

But maybe that's what she needs now—my help, before she ruins her life. The problem is, she believes in that theory like little kids believe in Santa Claus. I've tried to talk her out of it. She won't listen. All I've ever been able to do is sit back and make sure no asshole takes advantage of her. Now she's thinking about taking that away from me, too.

Fuming, I turn the doorknob and go inside. There's no helping Nora Reid.

Chapter Three

NORA

I clench my jaw and stab the key in the lock harder than I need to. I have no reason to be annoyed that Eli just called me predictable. I should take it as a compliment. Science is predictable. That's why I like it. It should not bother me that he'll be going to yet another party tonight, where he'll probably hook up with some lacrosse-loving fangirl. That's something we don't talk about—sex—though it's no secret he's a player. I mean, look at him.

I wouldn't be caught dead at Alex Koviak's party. It's not my crowd, plus Alex and I kissed at a party sophomore year, and that was the end of that. Worse, there's a largeish group of girls in school who don't like that I've dated and rejected so many guys. I used to be friends with a lot of them, but now they ignore me. The price of science.

This all translates into me not going to parties often, and honestly, I don't think I'm missing much. I usually feel guilty when Eli invites me—he *always* does—and I turn him down, but not today. That was a jerk comment he made, and he can suck it.

I throw open the front door and step inside.

The house is dark and cool and quiet and relaxes me immediately. Mom's at work and then she has class. She's going to be a dental hygienist this time. The times before it was masseuse, phlebotomist, and nail technician, none of which stuck. I hope one of her hypotheses work out soon.

On the way upstairs, I pass my grandparents' wedding picture and the sight of them comforts me. That's how sure I am of Maggie and Harold Frye and their incredible love story. I touch Gigi's face on the black-and-white print. She's beautiful, and while I never met him, I think Grandpa was a stone-cold fox. The look on his face, on both their faces... so content...always fills me with hope that my hypothesis is solid. That my own Harold is only a kiss away.

Up in my room, I flip open my laptop and go to Emory's site, trying to keep those embers of hope alive. They have one of the best medical research programs in the country, and I didn't think I'd get in. It's my dream school, but without scholarships, I can't go. That's why I haven't told anyone. Plus, my stomach twists when I think about leaving Mom and Gigi.

And then there's Eli.

My face heats up again when I think of that snarky comment in his truck.

He infuriates me, which wouldn't bother me so much if I didn't still have this pesky crush on him. It's like a bite that itches the more I scratch it.

For example, right now, I hear the Costases's garage door go up. I run into my bathroom, step into the bathtub, and stand on my toes to see through the small window.

I can't stop myself, and I don't even try. I've been doing this for years.

There he is, on the driveway, lugging a container of

recyclable plastic to the curb. He's changed his clothes from school. Now he's wearing that sea-green T-shirt that makes his eyes even bluer. When he heads back inside, I sink down into the empty tub and hold my head in my hands. I'm pathetically obsessed with my completely off-limits best friend. I mean, how many times have I imagined him here, in this pink-tiled bathroom? He comes in from lacrosse practice, hot and sweaty. I turn on the shower, pull that jersey up, over his head. My fingers trail along his tanned chest, my lips follow…

It's a harmless fantasy. Right?

I'm not so sure.

What if this stupid crush is affecting my test results? How can I experience the perfect first kiss if I'm imagining myself doing things with Eli that best friends don't normally do?

I run a hand through my hair, my awesome new, celebratory hair, and climb out of the bathtub. Enough of this. I march back into my room, grab my pie and laptop, and plop onto my bed. First things first, get my emotions in check. I take a bite of pie…and instantly cringe. The crust is mushy and the filling is way too sweet. Bad pie fixes nothing!

Scowling, I open the scholarship page on the Emory website, click on the first application, and get to work. I'd be stupid not to try.

After an hour or so of filling out forms, I hear the signature asthmatic cough of Eli's truck attempting to come to life. I focus even harder on the screen. *I will not run to the window. I will not run to the window.* And I don't.

My chest fills with pride. There, see? I can control myself.

I feel kind of bad, though. He drives around in that wreck while I have a perfectly good car that Gigi bought me for my sixteenth birthday sitting in the garage.

I close my laptop as Eli tries the ignition again. Probably going to the party early. Every girl there will want him. Will any of them succeed?

I imagine him here, next to me, in my bed, smiling, with that damn dimple. We face each other, knowing what we both want…

NO!

I have to think of something else. *Anything* else.

I roll onto my back and gaze at the stick-on constellations on my ceiling that have been there since I was little. I've always loved science, everything about it. I've always wanted to help people, animals, the planet. Emory could make all that possible in a big way.

Finally, the truck starts. Michael Jordan. Who names their truck? It's actually kind of cute.

Oh my God, not even science can distract me. Frantically, I take another bite of the subpar pie. Its over-sweetness coats my tongue with a sour taste, but hey, at least I'm thinking about something else for a second. I close the container and toss it into the trash can next to my desk. So much for pie fixing everything.

I desperately want to have that kiss, to meet the One, but what if I'm missing the signs because I can't stop fantasizing about Eli? In my shower. In my bed. In Michael Jordan. Under the bleachers at school. There is nowhere I haven't imagined Eli and me together.

This has been going on for way too long. It's time for a change.

I run my fingers through my curls again and know what I have to do.

Not that we won't be friends anymore. I just need to break the Eli habit. There are three months to graduation, and there are still guys to kiss and possible scholarships to acquire. My car has been sitting in the garage since I hit the driver's ed instructor two years ago and broke her leg. I can still hear the crunch and the bloodcurdling scream. I haven't driven since.

Truth is, I'm terrified to get behind the wheel. I just can't think of a better way to distance myself from Eli than to stop letting him drive me around every day. The only glitch: I need someone to teach me, and unfortunately, I think he's the only one who can.

Two weeks. That's my plan—two weeks to get over my driving anxiety and get some refresher lessons from Eli. Then I won't need him anymore. I can move on to other boys, and maybe Emory, then we can really be just friends.

The next morning, I hear the *thonk*ing sound of the basketball on his driveway. Great. He's awake. I force myself not to think of his bed head, or his probably shirtless chest. I need to stay focused if this plan is going to work. Mom can't teach me how to drive. She made me crazy last time, always gasping and pushing imaginary brake pedals. Abby is always busy. Gigi can't teach me anymore. It's Eli or no one.

I head outside in the T-shirt I slept in and pajama pants. Oh.

I turn in a circle and consider going back inside because I was right. He's not wearing a shirt. Honestly, why does he have to tempt me like this?

What really makes me breathless, though, which I am right now, is when he wears his glasses. I don't know what it is about those things. They're just big, black retro-looking frames, and they are seriously killing me.

I throw my shoulders back and make my way toward him anyway, determined.

Just ask him the favor. Stick to the plan.

"Eli," I start, but his little brother, Ari, runs out their back door before I can finish. I love Ari. He's eleven, a sixth grader, and even though he's Eli's brother, he's like mine, too.

"Nora Reid." He likes to greet people with their full names. He runs over like he might hug me, and then he doesn't. That's okay.

"Ari Costas." I tip my head toward Eli, who is holding the ball. "You showing him how to play?"

"Yes," Ari agrees. "I'm showing him how to play."

Eli smirks. "In your dreams, butthead."

That smirk is so cute it makes me woozy. I swallow hard. "Pass it, Costas." I clap my hands. "And how about maybe put a shirt on?"

"Why? You can't handle this?" He throws me the ball and the action makes his pecs flex. I shake my head. God, he's beautiful.

I watch the ground and dribble the ball. *Focus!* "Where are your contacts?"

"Girls like when he wears his glasses," Ari says matter-of-factly.

I laugh out loud. Yes, Eli is as hot as the surface of Mercury, but he knows it. This fact brings me back to earth. "Oh," I say, "is that so? A bare chest and hipster glasses and we're falling at your feet. You really think that works?"

It does. It so works.

He grins. "I don't know. You're looking a little wobbly."

"You wish." I lift the ball, aim, and arc it toward the net for a resounding miss.

He nabs the rebound and tosses it back to me. "Come on, Reid, aim for the box!"

He's given me this advice about a million times over the years. "I am, Coach!" Which is not even remotely true. The next time, I aim for the stupid box and voilà, it goes in.

"See?" he says smugly. "Maybe I *am* more than just a pretty face." He pushes the glasses up on his nose. I try to hide the shudder that ripples through me. He's a pretty face, and more. He's just not my pretty face, and never can be.

That's why you're out here, Nora!

I clear my throat and cross my arms. "Eli?"

"Yeah?" he says. "Hey, what's up with your hair anyway?"

"What?" I touch it. Oh God, I didn't even look at it before I ran outside. The humidity. It's got to be huge.

He lifts a hand and waves it around. "It's like, everywhere."

My insides clench. He doesn't like my hair? I immediately corral it into a ponytail. "I just got up. Jeez."

"No, I mean, it's not bad," he says. "It's just different."

Ari walks to his brother and takes the ball from him. "He likes your hair. He thinks your hair is pretty."

The world goes silent. Because the thing about Ari is, he doesn't lie. He's wonderful and brilliant and funny, and he's on the autism spectrum, which is another medical mystery I'd like to research. Ari is sensitive to emotions and sounds, remembers all sorts of facts about things like weather and sports, and he never, ever lies.

"What the fuh—?" Eli catches himself, and his face goes blank. "I did not say that."

I smile at Ari while my mind whirls like one of those paper pinwheels in the wind. "He does, does he?"

"Yes. And he also wants to kiss you."

I swallow hard and say nothing.

Eli's tanned face reddens, I swear it does. "Uh. What? There is no way in hell." He lifts his chin to me. "No offense."

Now my face gets hot. "Oh, don't worry, none taken." Although I'm not going to lie, I've totally taken offense. "No way" I understand. But "in hell"? That's a little extreme.

"Mom!" Ari shouts. "Eli said a bad word." He runs into the house to tell his mother.

A weird silence falls between Eli and me until he dribbles the ball. *Thonk*. "Just so you know, I never said that," he says.

Why would he say that? That ship sailed five years ago in Madison Dunn's garage. "I know."

He drills the ball hard into the driveway again, not making eye contact. "I mean, I'm not an idiot. I would never say that, or think it."

I scratch my head. That's enough of this conversation. "All right. I got it." Time to make my plan happen. "Hey, do you have time to head out to the center? Just for a short visit?"

His forehead wrinkles. "Now? I guess."

"Good." I bite my bottom lip. "Also, I was thinking maybe we could take my car?" I make fists of my hands—I'm more nervous than I thought. He dribbles the ball again. "And that maybe I can drive?" I almost whisper.

"You want to drive?"

I blink, not really wanting to drive at all. "Yeah. I mean, yes. I want to get my license. For real this time."

"*You?*" Two more *thonks* of the ball. "*Drive?*"

"God. Yes. Me. Drive." My mouth is dry and I sound like a caveman. "Look, it's not a big deal. I'm just ready, and I can't tell Mom. Not yet. She thinks I should never drive again."

He says nothing, like maybe he agrees with Mom.

I see he's going to take some convincing. "Just think. When I can drive, you'll be free of me. Here's your chance to get your life back."

He palms the ball back and forth between his hands, then drops it. *Thonk.* "I don't mind driving you around."

"I know, I know." I look toward our garage where the death trap awaits. "It's just that I'm eighteen. Realistically I need to be able to drive. Right?"

And also, maybe it'll help me stop picturing you naked in my bathtub?

When I glance up, his eyes are burning into me.

He drops the ball on the driveway and it rolls away. "Okay, but if you hit something—or some*one*—I'm out. Like, I will flee the scene. You'll be on your own."

I frown. "Thanks. That really helps my confidence."

Eli inhales deep. "Okay. Grab your keys, Dale Jr."

"Who?"

He rubs his forehead. "Never mind. Get dressed and let's go."

Chapter Four

She wants driving lessons? The second she puts it out there, I know why. My stomach drops. This is about Emory University and all the new guys she'll be able to kiss.

Dammit, she's actually seriously considering that place.

Also, thanks to my brother, she now thinks I want to kiss her. I know it's not Ari's fault that he just says things, but that doesn't mean I don't want to kill him.

For reasons I can't comprehend, I agree to go with her to see Gigi. Up in my bathroom, I get ready like it's a damn date. It's hot for February, so I body spray the crap out of every crevice, get dressed, and start to put in contacts. Then I stop, remember something Nora said a while back, about how she loves guys in glasses.

She was talking about some actor, I can't even remember who. She said, "He's not that cute in real life, but he puts on those glasses and I swear, I'd do anything for him."

Anything.

Although she wouldn't, would she? Not if she kissed him first and it sucked. She'd just add him to her list of unlovable dudes.

I scowl at myself in the bathroom mirror. God, do I really think girls like these stupid things? Do I think that *she* likes them?

Don't be a dumbass. That girl doesn't care how you look. She's spent the last five years reminding me that I have absolutely no place in her messed-up plan for future happiness. Meanwhile, I've spent the last five years trying to move on, all while watching her date and dump a string of guys who didn't measure up. According to Nora, we're two people who kissed once, badly. End of story. After that, she stuck me in the friend zone, where I've hung out ever since.

That's when the idea hits me like a lacrosse shaft to the shin. What if one of us first-kiss losers escape the friend zone? Changed her mind? Proved her theory wrong? Maybe she wouldn't want to go to Emory. Maybe she'd stay in Edinburgh.

What if she fell for someone she crossed off her list a long time ago?

Someone like me. No one else could pull it off. No one knows her like I do.

Just like that, I have a plan.

The five miles to and from school every weekday isn't enough time to make it happen, but giving her driving lessons changes things. We'll have to spend more time together. We'll have to go places, besides school and home, together.

I will make Nora Reid fall in love with me.

I slip the glasses back on and try to ignore how totally impossible that sounds.

She's in the garage talking to Ari when I come down. He's comfortable with her, more than he is with most people. Sometimes I wonder if, deep down, *he* has a crush on Nora. I'm pretty sure he doesn't really understand love or romance, but what do I know? Ari's got a lot of secrets locked inside that brain of his. He's super smart, so smart that I'm pretty sure my parents wonder how the hell they ended up with a dumbshit like me.

Ari would hate it if she left. I'm doing this for him, too.

"Can I go with you?" he asks Nora. "I've never been in a 2015 Ford Escort."

"You have karate today, numbnuts," I remind him.

"Ah-yah!" He chops through the air. This kid. I love the dude.

"All right, calm down, Chuck Norris. Go inside. Mom wants you."

A turd-like grin spreads across his face. "You're going on a date."

Dammit, I'm gonna kill him.

Nora spits out a laugh. "No, we're not, Ari. Not in a million years." She catches my gaze and sneers. "No offense," she says. Those eyes sparkle.

It sucks having your own words thrown back in your face.

"None taken," I say. She hands me the keys and I'm confused. "I thought you were driving?"

She walks around to the passenger side and gets in without a word. I get behind the steering wheel and close the door behind me. "What's going on?" I ask. "You aren't gonna drive?"

"Yes, I'm going to drive," she says. "Just not here. Mom's inside."

I nod. "Oh that's right, I forgot we're perpetrating a lie. Will she mind that I'm driving your car?"

"I told her we wanted to see Gigi," she says, "and that MJ

isn't exactly reliable."

I stick the key into the ignition. It never leaves the garage, so I guess it makes sense that it still smells like new car. It purrs like a kitten when I turn the key. Not like Michael Jordan. Of course, MJ has heart, and this thing is pretty much a soulless shell of generic steel.

I back down the driveway. "He's not unreliable."

I don't have to look at her to know she's smirking.

"Not at all," she says with maximum sarcasm.

"When are we switching places?"

"I don't know—the Mermaid?"

Fine. I drive us there in silence, feeling like this plan of mine hasn't got a chance in hell. When I pull into the Mermaid and put the car in park, she gulps, loudly.

"You sure you want to do this?" I ask. "You look sort of pale."

She hesitates, blinks slowly. "Yes. I'm sure." Doesn't sound convincing at all. "It's time. It's definitely time."

I run my hands along the top of the steering wheel. "Why? No one's forcing you."

She gnaws on her bottom lip. That's her tell when she's worried. "No, I know." But she doesn't make a move to get out.

"You sick of me?" I ask.

She turns to face me. "No. Of course not. I just need to do this. It's time." Her eyes, they're so big. "Will you help me?"

I feel a twist in my chest, like an overturned screw, and something inside me breaks. Damn this girl and the power she holds over me. I reach for the door handle. "Let's switch."

She doesn't move.

"You know," I say, "if you want to get a driver's license, you might actually have to drive." I'm relieved that I can still be a sarcastic son of a bitch, even when I'm a total pushover to this girl who is keeping a huge secret from me.

"Okay," she says, so quiet I almost can't hear her. "Just don't make fun of me." She hesitates, then opens her door. "Promise."

"I don't know. I'll try?"

There's a half smile, but by the time we trade places, it's gone. It's pretty much just sheer terror on her face.

"You all right?" I ask.

Tiny nod.

"You know, if you puke, you can kiss this new car smell good-bye forever."

She grips the steering wheel. "You couldn't even get out of the parking lot without making fun of me."

I set my jaw. "Okay, right, sorry, sorry."

"You know," she says. "A pep talk, maybe, might be good."

"Okay. Right." I've been playing lacrosse since I was four. Pep talks I can do. "Hey, Nora?"

She stares blankly out the windshield like she's stoned. Damn, she's really freaked out.

"Nora? Yo. Look at me."

She turns my way. There she is. Terrified.

I put on my serious game face. "So, there's nothing to this driving thing. It's easy."

Her gaze moves back out the front window.

"Eyes on me, Reid," I say. "Listen. To successfully drive a car, you have to do two things: one"—I hold up a finger—"stay in the lines, just like in kindergarten. Remember, coloring? Stay in the lines. And Two." I add another finger. "Don't hit the car in front of you. That's pretty much all there is to it."

"That is not all there is," she says.

"Well…" I dip my chin. "True. You should also look behind you when you back up so you don't break anyone's legs. I'm guessing you won't forget to do that again, though.

Right?"

She sits up straighter. "No. I won't. Right."

"Okay. You remember which pedal is which?"

She hits me with her angry eyes, still huge and sparkling. "I do have a functioning brain."

"I know, but it's been a while. You gotta adjust your mirrors. Can you do that?"

"Yeah, I think so," she says and reaches for the rearview. She runs the little automatic side mirror switch and then turns back to me. "Okay."

I slap the dashboard. "Great. Okay, let's go."

She looks over her right shoulder, puts the car in reverse, and starts to slowly back up. And by slowly I mean she's not moving at all.

"You gotta give it some gas."

"I know. Just…give me a second."

I'm trying to stay calm, but I'm starting to think maybe this was a bad idea.

"It's all right." I keep my voice low. "I get it. Just get past the first back up and you'll be gold."

She breathes deep again and steps on the gas. The car jerks, but eventually she finds the sweet spot and manages to back out in a perfect arc.

"Nice." I turn around. "Don't see any bone shards."

"Shut up." She shifts into drive and maneuvers slowly through the parking lot.

"Good. You're really doing good. You feel better?" I ask. She was almost done with driver's ed when the accident happened. She *knows* how to drive. It just freaked her out, which is why her mom has paid me to drive her to school for almost two years.

"Yeah, sort of." She tries for a confident expression, but doesn't quite hit the mark.

Coach once made the team do yoga together, so I try to

channel what I remember. "Just stay calm. You're doing fine."

She turns onto Main Street and gets honked at almost immediately.

She squeals. "Why are they honking at me? Idiots!"

"That's it," I say. "Embrace the road rage. Use it. Maybe to push the gas pedal?" She's totally crawling.

"I asked you not to make fun of me," she says.

"Sorry. Sorry. You're doing great, just a little more gas. Please."

She guns it so she's actually going the speed limit, for about thirty seconds.

I don't say anything.

It takes us twice as long as it should to get to Edinburgh Oaks Assisted Living Center. Nora stays about five miles an hour below the posted speed limit the entire time, and passes the entrance twice. She parks the car like she's legally blind, but the lot is mostly empty so I don't make a big deal of it.

I don't think this plan is gonna work.

She uncurls her fingers from the steering wheel. It's like they're shrink-wrapped to the leather. "Okay," she says. "I did it. That wasn't too bad, was it?" Her body visibly relaxes. "Thanks, Eli. What would I do without you?"

"You'd be totally fucked."

She frowns. "I hate that word."

"Sometimes it's the only one that works."

We get out of the car and walk side by side to the front doors. The building looks like a hospital, it's a dull beige color with two floors. As usual, there are a bunch of really old people on the benches out front, or in wheelchairs, a lot of them in pajamas. Most of them smile, some of them wave. I wave back at one old guy sitting right by the door. He's thinking, *This is you one day, sonny boy!*

Nora leads the way through the automatic doors and I'm hit with the usual smell—shit and cough syrup.

"God, can't they do something about that?" I cough. She signs us in and I follow her down the wide hall. I've been to visit more than a few times, and I try not to let this place or these people creep me out. But it does. And they do. Because that dude outside is right. This is where we're all headed, and that's depressing as hell.

We get to room 116, and Nora raps lightly on the door.

"Come on in," a voice, not Gigi's, says.

Nora pushes the door open and there she is, sitting in her chair, with her nurse, Claudia, brushing her hair.

What happens next is anyone's guess. Sometimes Gigi remembers us, sometimes she doesn't. Nora gets really sad when she doesn't, so I hope for the best.

There's something about Nora being sad that, since the day we met, makes me nuts. There's nothing I can do about Gigi, but with my new plan, I might be able to save Nora from future sadness as a lonely cat lady.

All I have to do is make her question everything she believes, get her to fall for me, denounce her dumbass first kiss theory, and now, make sure she doesn't kill us both in a car accident.

Sure. No problem.

Chapter Five

"Hey, look who's here, Miss Maggie," Claudia says. "It's Nora and Eli, come for a visit."

Gigi lifts her head. *God, let her remember me*, I send up a silent prayer. Eli is beside me, and I almost reach for his hand, but stop myself in the nick of time.

Gigi smiles big. "Oh, there's my sweet Nora and Eli."

I almost sag with relief. Instead, I make a beeline for her. "Hi, Gigi!"

I give her a hug, noticing how thin she feels in my arms. Then it's Eli's turn. He and Gigi have always been close, even before I moved in, and her smile gets even wider as his broad shoulders engulf her.

"We're having a good day today," Claudia reports. "This young lady ate all her lunch, and she played a game of checkers with Mr. Ruiz."

Gigi huffs. "Well, I was hungry! And that man was getting way too cocky about his checker-playing abilities."

"Did you whoop his ass?" Eli asks.

"You better believe I did," she says, sounding like her old self.

I pull up a chair beside her. "Did you have a good week?" I ask.

She takes my hand and pats it. "Oh yes. I miss my sweet girl, though."

My heart hurts in my chest. "I miss you, too." I try to keep my voice from breaking. I'm here to cheer her up, not to cry.

"Grades good?"

"Of course," I say.

She pats my hand again and turns to Claudia. "Nora is number one in her class. She's going to be a scientist." I'm glad she remembers that fact, if only she hadn't told Claudia the same exact thing when I was here last week.

Claudia nods enthusiastically, pretending not to notice. "Yes, that's so exciting. You know where you're going to college yet?"

My eyes slide toward Eli. "Um. State, to start." He has no reaction, of course, because to him, that's still the plan. He doesn't know things might change.

"Nothing wrong with State," Claudia says. That's what everyone says about State—and I know she's right. It's close, and you have to take all those basic classes no matter where you go, so why go somewhere that costs more? It makes sense.

"Did you hear from that other school?" Gigi asks. "What was it?"

Crap. I told her about Emory when I came to visit her after the new year. I didn't think she'd remember.

"Nah. Hey, Gigi, you wanna play some Go Fish?" *Smooth, Nora. Way to lie to your grandmother.* There's a special place in hell for people who do that.

"Sure. Go Fish sounds fun."

I run to get the cards in her drawer.

"Now who are you?" Gigi asks. She's talking to Eli. He glances at me, a crease between those blue eyes.

He takes the deck from me without missing a beat. "It's me, Gigi, it's Eli." He cuts the cards and starts to shuffle. "I stopped by to make sure you're not causing too much trouble." He winks at her, and smiles that smile that melts me to my core.

She giggles. "Oh, what fun would it be if I wasn't causing trouble?" She tilts her head and winks at him. "You're a handsome young man."

"Hey, thanks," he says. "You're not so bad yourself."

Gigi laughs out loud, and I calm down. Eli's lived next door to her his whole life. I know this isn't easy for him, either, but he handles it so well; much better than I do.

"Hey, you know what, Gigi?" I say. "I drove my car here today."

Her eyes narrow. "You did?"

"Yes, Eli's gonna give me lessons so I can finally get my license. I'll be able to come and see you more."

"Oh, wonderful," she says. "It's about time." She scolds me and I'm so happy, it's like she's her normal self. God, I hate this disease. I want to kill it, wipe it off the planet. Yet another reason to go to Emory.

Claudia brings us a plate of cookies and we play Go Fish. It's Gigi and me versus Eli, and he's letting us win.

We make it through one game when Claudia comes back and asks Gigi if she's tired.

She looks at me, then Eli. "Yes, I am. You come back and see me now, kids. You're both so sweet." Her eyes move between us, unfocused. "Tell me your name again."

Oh God, no. She talking to me. "It's me, Gigi. Nora."

"Oh." Her head wobbles back and forth. "Of course. Thank you for coming. You, too, young man."

I touch her hand. "Gigi, I'll see you next weekend, okay?" I am desperate for her to remember me. "I love you." I give her a hug and a kiss on the cheek. I can see that she's tired. She doesn't say I love you back.

Heartbroken, I shuffle out of there like a zombie. "She seemed thinner. Did she look thinner to you?"

Eli shrugs. "No. She looked good."

"Don't lie." We get into the car, me behind the wheel, and I start to cry. I'm not a crier, but right now I can't help it.

"Hey," he says. "It's gonna be okay."

I sniff and hope to God he's right. "I know, I know." I wipe my eyes. "Jeez, I hate crying. It's such a waste of time." I start the car. "I also *hate* driving."

He sighs. "You want me to drive home?"

I face front and clench my teeth. "No." I start the car, back up slowly. Too slow judging from Eli's body language, which is telling me he would really, really like to shout "Go!"

Eventually, I make it out of the spot and the car lurches forward through the parking lot. "I am so gonna need some pie," I say.

"Oh hell, yeah."

I finally hit the gas and start down the main road. Eli gets a text and stares at his phone. I haven't asked him about Koviak's party, but I know it got broken up around midnight by the cops. I laid in my bed, waiting for him to come home. He was still out when I fell asleep around one. So where was he? Who was he with?

These are exactly the things that are none of my business, and I should not care about. And why I need to get my driver's license.

We're moving along nicely, I think. I'm calm and breathing normally. Eli chuckles at his phone, and suddenly something darts out in front of me from the side of the road. My heart jumps into my throat. I scream and slam on the brakes. The car skids and squeals and Eli jerks forward, his phone flinging out of his hand.

"Oh no! No, no, no, no!" I yell.

"What happened?" he shouts.

I grab his T-shirt sleeve. "I hit it! I hit it! I *always* hit something!"

"What did you hit?"

I'm close to hyperventilating. "I don't know, something! Where is it?"

He looks behind us where cars are honking. "Dude! You can't stop like that out of nowhere. You could have killed us."

"Don't yell!" I squint, and in the middle of the lane in front of us, I spot a kitten. "Oh no! I hit a kitten!"

The honking behind us gets louder, but I don't care. I put the car in park, and run out into the street, waving my arms wildly, so none of these idiots trying to pass me hits the kitten. Again.

"Shit!" Eli shouts and hops out, too. "Nora, get back here! What are you doing? Get back in the car!"

The kitten isn't moving, but when I reach it in the road, it looks okay. I stick out my hand and it sniffs me, staring up with big black eyes as the cars behind us lay on their horns. The poor thing is terrified. I scoop it up and hold it to my chest, then hurry back to the car and shut myself inside. Eli gets back in, too, slamming the door.

"Do you want to die?" he yells. "Holy shit! Give that motherfucker to me and drive!"

"Don't call it that and stop yelling!"

He reaches out and takes it. "Just give it to me and go!"

"Does it look okay?"

He snarls. "Oh my God, would you *go*?"

I'm flustered with all the horns, so I hit the gas without putting the car in drive.

"Put it in drive!"

"Okay! Don't yell. It's already scared." I am, too, though I don't mention that. I put the car in gear and drive. The car jolts forward, but I only go as far as the gas station on the corner, where I pull in and park.

"What are you doing?" Eli asks.

I'm shaking as the kitten meows and squirms against his chest. "I can't do this. I can't drive."

I'll have to find some other way to get over Eli, because he's going to have to drive me around for the rest of the year. Maybe the rest of my life. Because I *cannot* do this.

And…I'm crying again. I hate my life.

"Nora," he says, his voice calmer now. "Come on, stop." The kitten meows again. "Don't lose it. Okay?"

I raise my hands in surrender. "No. Can't. Too late. I've already lost it. You saw Gigi. Eli, she's getting worse. And I can't drive a car without almost killing something." I grab the steering wheel, lean my forehead on it. "I *can't* do this."

"Wow," he says, holding the cat up in front of his face. "You hear that, cat? She's giving up."

The words stab me like a knife. I straighten up. "It's not giving up. It's facing facts. Driving is not a skill I can master. I'm sorry." I reach out and pet the cat on the head with one finger. I start crying again thinking I almost smashed it to oblivion.

He holds the kitten close to his chest. It's way too adorable.

He turns to face me. "Come on, Nor. Maybe look at this glass as half full, huh? I mean, Gigi remembered you today, and me, too, mostly, and then she got tired. That's all. She was tired. So it was a good visit. And you drove all the way out here. You did that. Yeah, you did it like a hundred-year-old blind person, but I don't think that's so bad for someone who hasn't been behind the wheel in two years. You can drive. And this dumbass cat got its own self stuck in the middle of the road. You didn't put it there. You saved it. I mean, even though you almost got us killed, you saved it. So if you wanna quit, quit. I'll drive you around next year. I don't mind. Twenty bucks a week buys my gas."

The kitten lets out a high-pitched meow.

I bite my bottom lip. "I don't know."

"What don't you know? You can do quantum physics, you can drive a damn car. Give yourself a chance. Let me give you some refresher lessons, except we're not just going to the center and back. Let's have fun, too. Okay?"

He's right. "I can't do quantum physics," I say, "but I won't quit." I put the car in drive. "Also, don't call my cat a dumbass."

I notice his smirk, which calms me, and I go.

We stop at the Mermaid to change places. The kitten is sound asleep against Eli's chest. I didn't have any more near misses, though my fingers are still molded to the steering wheel.

"What are you gonna do with it?" Eli nods down at the ball of fluff in his hands.

"I don't know. I'm not sure what Mom will say."

We get out, and as he walks around the front of the car, I notice him flinch when he takes a step with his right leg.

"Does your knee hurt?"

He flexes it as he hands me the cat. "Nah, it's good. I just stepped wrong when I was trying to save your life *in the middle of the street*." He adds a half-hearted glare for good measure.

I stick my tongue out at him. Problem is, I don't know if he's being honest. I'm not a big lacrosse fan, but I know that he's an attackman, he's the team captain, and he's good. Sophomore year, he tore his right ACL and had to have surgery, then didn't play for the rest of the season. It took him a while to get back, and he's got a spot on the team at State next year.

He loves lacrosse and if he can't play, I have no idea what he'll do. I'm afraid it might involve living with his parents until he's forty.

I search his eyes and feel my heart respond. I worry about him probably more than I should. "You're not pushing it, are you?"

"No. It's just a little stiff. I'll know if I need to get it checked."

He drives us home as I hold the kitten, gray and wriggling, on my lap.

Eli glances over. "So, you want more lessons?" he says as he pulls back into my garage.

In the quiet car, it feels like something passes between us, something unspoken, but understood. This isn't the first time this has happened—a moment when it almost seems like he can read my mind.

Then the moment passes, and I remind myself that he cannot read my mind, and if he could, it would be a disaster. He'd know that a big part of me wants him to drive me around forever, which is exactly why I need to get my license.

"Yes," I say. "Please."

He lifts a corner of his mouth. "Okay. Party, Friday. At the beach. You're driving."

Panic hits me. That's a few days from now. "Wait. What?"

"It's perfect. No lacrosse practice and no school on Friday. I'm free. You're free. No excuses."

He gets out of the car and shuts the door before I can protest. Smart of him, since there's no way I'm going to that party.

Chapter Six

ELI

I limp in from practice on Thursday, glad I have a day off tomorrow to rest my knee. The locker room reeks of sweaty pinnies and jockstraps. It's a smell that makes most people want to hurl. Not me, though. It's just part of the game, and as far as I'm concerned, there's nothing bad about lacrosse.

We take a lot of shit from other athletes who say we're just a bunch of rich, white assholes, but we've got all kinds of kids on our team. Black, white, Hispanic. We've got Sam Liu, the best goalie in central Florida. We've got rich kids like Alex Koviak—he's got a trust fund. Middle-class kids like me. Dad's the police chief and does okay, but he's also a cheap ass who believes in making his kids work for things. I bought MJ with my own lawn mowing money. Then there are the Ponti brothers—their mom is Donna the waitress at the Mermaid, and they live in the trailer park on the way out of town. They're pretty much always broke. All these guys, though, no matter what, give 150 percent on the field, and together we're more than a team, we're brothers.

Koviak comes over as I'm getting dressed. "Hey, dickweed," he says. He likes to act like an asshole, but I've known him a long time and it's mostly just show. He's a good guy. "What's wrong with you? You played like shit today."

I want to punch him. "Fuck off. Nothing's wrong." That's not entirely true, my bad knee is stiff. It's not that bad, it just makes me paranoid. I can't have any more injuries. If it keeps up, I'll have to let someone know.

"Better not be." Koviak shakes his head, throwing sweat everywhere with his shaggy-ass hair. "I need a good season this year."

I grab my towel and slam my locker shut. "Yeah, we all do," I say. I've already committed to State but I'm not taking anything for granted. My season last year was shaky after the injury, and I'm lucky they still want me.

"You're coming tomorrow, yeah?" Koviak asks.

The beach party. I nod. "Yeah, I'll be there." I still can't believe I got Nora to agree to go. Not that I gave her much choice. If my plan is gonna work, we need to spend time *together.*

"Cool, cool," he says. "There's someone there that I want you to meet."

I groan because Koviak, in spite of his fake douchiness, also has a reputation as the romantic of the team. He likes to play matchmaker, too, which can be annoying as hell.

"It's all right, Alex. Thanks, but no thanks."

He pushes my shoulder. "What? No, you don't wanna meet a smokin' hot chick? Dude, she's a junior at Cross Creek. She's seen you play, man. Wants to meet you."

Koviak means well, I know that. The last girl he set me up with, though...she had some serious issues, bordering on stalker territory. "No. I'm just gonna ride out the rest of the year. No more set ups, okay?"

"I mean it, man. She's like, made for you."

He's not giving up. I laugh at his serious face. "How is she *made* for me? Have you even met her?"

He leans against the lockers. "No, but I've seen her Snapchat stories. She loves lacrosse players. Like, *loves* them, loves them." His eyebrows jump up and down.

"Then you go out with her. I've already got plans."

He smacks my arm. "No shit," he says, "you bringing someone?"

I give him a shove back. "No. Not like that. We're just going together. Driving together. To the beach. In the same car."

"Who, man, who?"

Tex walks in, towel wrapped around his middle. "Mind if I... I just need to get to my locker," he says with that southern drawl. He's new, just transferred from somewhere in Texas. I can't remember his real name, and I don't know him well, but he seems okay. We move out of his way.

Koviak smacks his own forehead. "Wait. Hold on. No. You are not talking about who I think you're talking about. Not Nora."

I scowl at him in warning. "Yeah."

"Dude, what is it with you? You know how she rolls. You are cemented in the friend zone with her, my brother. As in, not going anywhere, ever."

I close my locker with a bang, hoping to drown him out. "We're going. As friends."

For now.

"Don't mean to listen in"—Tex says over his shoulder—"but are you talking about Nora Reid?"

Koviak watches me while addressing Tex. "Listen, Tex, don't even think about it. Trust me, go after her and you'll end up with the bluest of balls."

Anger flares in my chest. "Shut up, Alex. She's my friend."

"E," Koviak says, "you have to admit, no one gets anywhere with her." He turns to Tex. "Trust me, many have tried."

Tex ignores Koviak and turns to me. "You know her pretty well, Eli?"

"Yeah." It's weird, I don't like talking about Nora like this. "She's my neighbor."

"Huh." He raises his chin, runs a hand through his hair, which isn't easy since it's a buzz cut. Must be a hockey thing. Word is he played back in Texas, and now he's giving lacrosse a try.

He squints at me. "So you're not into her?" he asks.

"Me?" I force myself to say no. Just because I'm trying to get her to fall in love with me doesn't mean I'm into her.

Or maybe it does, but it's complicated.

He smiles, and I almost flip my shit. "Good to hear. She's in AP bio with me," he drawls on. "Damn, that girl is smart. Funny. Cute. I just don't want to step on anyone's toes."

Kov pats his shoulder. "Listen, Caleb. I'm telling you, let me work my magic. I'll set you up with a girl who you can actually get somewhere with. Nora's too serious. Uptight. Don't waste your time." He turns his attention to me. "And you"—he points—"I don't care if you bring her. I'm just saying if you do, the odds of getting laid tomorrow night drastically decrease."

"Thanks, I'm pretty sure I'll survive." I pull my shirt over my head.

"Just trying to help!" he shouts and heads for the showers.

"Douchebag," I mumble and grab my bag. Tex chuckles. He shouldn't.

I close my locker and glance at his bare back. He's cut. Steroids probably. I guess he's smart, too, in that AP class with Nora, and he's interested in her, which pisses me off.

"So…" He turns and catches my glare. "Nora'll be at the

beach tomorrow?"

"Yeah," I say. "With me."

"Just not *with* you."

Jackass. I mean, I know I said he's a good guy but right now I want to rip his throat out.

"Yeah." That's one thing I didn't take into consideration in my plot to take down the first kiss hypothesis: other guys.

If this is gonna happen, her attention has to be on me—on *us*. I've got to make it so she won't even *want* to kiss anyone new. She's got to want me, even though our first kiss sucked. Her hypothesis will be blown to bits. She'll have to admit she's been wrong all along.

It's genius, my plan, and there's no place in it for this asshole.

"You know," Tex muses. "I bet she's just waiting for the right guy. She just hasn't met her match—yet."

I tell myself to relax. "Sure." He's not exactly a threat. Still, when I gather up my things to leave, I brush past him and have to fight the urge to body slam him into the lockers.

When I get home, Nora's sitting in the middle of her driveway with Ari and the cat that she almost slaughtered in the road. Her mom is letting it hang out until Nora finds another home for it. She claims to be trying, but as far as I can tell, that's a lie.

"Hey," she says when I walk over.

I think of her with Tex and cringe. "Hey," I say back. "Hey, Ari." I turn to my brother. "You have a good day at school?"

"Yeah." He's petting the cat gently.

"What's up with the furball?"

Nora beams. "We took it to the vet and got it vaccinated."

"It's a girl," Ari says, holding it up and looking into its eyes. "Aren't you a girl? Yes, you're a girl." Ari doesn't really show affection to people, but he loves animals.

It makes me happy to see him respond to it. "Did you name it?" I ask Nora.

She pouts. "Mom doesn't think we should keep it."

"Why not?"

"Can I have it?" Ari doesn't waste a second to ask.

I stick my hands in my front pockets. "We're dog people, Ari," I say, and then turn to Nora. "Why won't she let you keep it?"

She shrugs. "Money. Pets aren't free, you know," she mimics her mom. "I'm not caving that easy. If no one claims her, she's mine."

"If not, can I have her?" Ari says.

"Ari, chill," I say. "Chester will eat that thing alive."

Ari's face freezes in fear. "He will? That's disgusting."

"Yeah, it would be. Now, Reid." I tap her knee with the end of my shoe. She looks up at me, dark-red hair framing those eyes. Damn. I need a second.

"What?" she asks.

The second passes and I'm back on task. "You're driving to the beach tomorrow, don't forget."

A huge sigh escapes her. "I don't think I can. I told Mr. Stokes that I'd come in tomorrow to help with the book drive."

I dig my hands deeper into my pockets and rock back and forth on my toes. I knew she'd do this. "No, no way. That's not happening. I mean, unless Stokes gives you a ride to school, and I don't think the single male school librarian is supposed to be picking up students to help with his 'book drive.'"

Her upper lip curls. "You're gross. He's like sixty. And gay."

"So? Still wouldn't look good. Let Stokes plan his own

book drive. It's your day off and you're driving me to the beach."

"Can I come?" Ari asks.

"No, dude, not this time."

Nora pulls her knees up to her chin and wraps her arms around them. "What if I just don't feel like going?"

"Come on, Reid. You have *got* to loosen up."

Poison darts shoot out of her eyes. Or they might as well be the way she's looking at me.

"It's been a long time," she says. "Most of those girls hate me."

Probably, but I don't want to ruin things by confirming it. "Come on. Don't be such a drama queen. They don't hate you. They just haven't spent time with you in a while. I mean, what's to hate?"

She gapes, so I keep going. "You're fun. Hilarious when you want to be. Put yourself out there again, or at least try. I'm just saying, it won't kill you. You might even have a good time. Plus, you want to practice driving, right?"

Her body deflates a little. "Can't we just go to the mall or something?"

I hang my head. Nothing about her is easy. "You think Eli Costas just sits around waiting to give you driving lessons? Eli Costas is a busy man, sweetheart."

She inhales. Ari lets the cat go and it pounces on some imaginary prey.

"Okay. I'll do it. I'll go."

What? Did I actually convince her? I'm in shock.

"Really? Okay. Good. Tomorrow, then. Like eleven?"

"Yes, eleven. Just promise you'll stop referring to yourself in the third person." She puts a hand out for the kitten. "And don't call me sweetheart." She rubs her fingers together and makes a kissing sound with her mouth. "Come here, Marie."

"Marie? I thought you didn't name it," I say.

She catches the kitten up in her hands and holds it to her chin, gives it a kiss on the nose. I'm weirdly jealous. "Well, I did. That's her name," she says.

"She's named after Marie Curie," my know-it-all brother chimes in. "Discovered radium." He rolls his eyes at Nora, who rolls her eyes at him, sending each other a signal that they think I'm a total know-nothing moron.

I sneer. "That's a dumb name."

"Right." Nora smiles. "We wouldn't expect you to understand." She lifts her free hand to Ari, who gives her a resounding high-five.

"Real loyal," I say to my brother. He doesn't pick up on the sarcasm. Nora chuckles, pushes herself up, and walks toward her house.

"Eleven o'clock, Reid," I shout after her. "Mom's packing a cooler. Bring a towel. Wear a swimsuit. Don't even think about trying to weasel out of it."

She waves. "Never."

That's not true. She'll try again tomorrow morning, but I don't care. I'll do whatever it takes to make sure it's the perfect day, that she has a great time, and that she can't wait to do it again.

Step one of my plan is underway.

Chapter Seven

NORA

When Mom gets home just after ten that night, I'm in the kitchen in my bikini, making cinnamon rolls. I don't have Gigi's pie-making skills—or any baking skills, really—but I can pop a tube of dough and shove it in the toaster oven easy enough.

Mom bursts out laughing when she sees me. "A bikini? I didn't get the memo. Or are swimsuits optional?"

It makes me happy to see her happy. It's been a rough few months around here. "I was just trying it on." More like trying to talk myself into actually going to this beach party. Yes, if I want my license and some semblance of freedom from Eli, I need to practice driving. I'm just not sure seeing Eli bare-chested all day is going to help my cause. "You hungry?"

She *tsks*, shaking her head. "Ugh. So many carbs. But yes. I'm starving."

"Did you have a good day?"

She's the PE aide at the elementary school and most days

she's ready to drop, and that's *before* she heads out to the community college to practice scraping plaque off people's teeth.

"Yes, the kids were crazy today. I did pass my gum disease exam, though, so that's good."

"That's great," I say. "And also gross."

"Oh, it was." She plops down on one of the red vinyl chairs that surround Gigi's vintage kitchen table. "Both of those things."

I stick the pan in the toaster oven, set the timer for ten minutes, and stare up at the wall behind the real oven. It's soot-colored from the smoke of the fire Gigi started when she was baking a pie and left the potholder inside. We cleaned up the mess as best we could, but we don't have the money to repair the damage, and the oven is dead.

"You still liking it—the teeth, I mean?"

She screws up her mouth. "There are good days and bad days. I do think I'm going to like it as a job, though. Plus it's good money. God knows we need it."

Money is the biggest worry around here. Gigi's retirement fund is paying for the assisted living center, but I know Mom's afraid it'll run out. Even though State is cheap for college, I know it weighs on her. A scholarship to Emory might erase that worry, except that it would add another one—I'd be leaving her on her own.

Her mood is souring. I have to fix that. "I'll be working this summer. Don't worry, I have a lot saved, and Dad will pitch in for school."

She blows a raspberry. "Sweetie, I wouldn't count on that."

My shoulders slump. "No, Mom. The last time I talked to him he said he had some money saved, and I didn't even bring it up." I know very well, though, that my father isn't known for keeping his promises when it comes to money.

"It'll work out. Somehow," she says.

Marie zips into the room, like she knew we needed some comic relief. She attacks the strap of Mom's purse, and we both crack up.

Mom watches the cat, then looks at me. "Do we have a cat now, honey?"

I give her a pleading smile. "I don't know, do we?"

"Well." She leans an elbow on the table, rests her chin in her hand. "I guess since you'll be living here next year, you'll be around to take care of it."

Living here. Right. Crap.

Nothing's ever easy.

She bends down and takes off her ugly dental hygienist shoes. "So, no school tomorrow? Plans?" She gets up and pours herself a glass of wine. "Please tell me they have something to do with a bikini?"

I wrap my arms around my middle. "A group of kids is going in to help with the book drive."

Her eyebrows draw together. "In their swimsuits?"

"No. This is for…" I clear my throat. "Eli invited me to some party the team is having at the beach, but I don't know."

She watches me. "You don't know what?"

I bite my bottom lip, not sure of my answer. "I just haven't been to any parties in a while, and you know there's probably going to be drinking."

"Are *you* going to drink?"

"No! I don't drink, Mom."

"Well, there was that one time."

My body stiffens remembering what an idiot I was. "Yeah, I know." That one time sophomore year. I was at Abby's house and her older brother had a bottle of vodka in his bedroom. We mixed it up with some orange juice and the next thing I remember was puking my brains out in her toilet. Her mom called my mom and it was pretty clear what we'd done. Mom was mad at me, but not as mad as I was at myself. I don't like to lose control.

I shudder at the memory. "Right. The one and only time. Never again. Trust me."

"I do trust you, honey. You should definitely go."

Wait. How did that happen? I don't even want to go.

She takes a sip of wine and sits back down. "What about Eli? He's driving. Will he be drinking?"

I lift a shoulder and take the opportunity to turn this in my favor. "Maybe. Probably. I don't know what he does when he's with them."

She smirks. "Hmm. Well if you tell him not to drink, he won't."

My jaw drops and I laugh. "Eli? Are you kidding? He never listens to me!"

The timer on the toaster oven dings. I take out the rolls, still gooey in the middle, just the way I like them. The smell of warm cinnamon wafts up around me, and I'm hit with a huge wave of missing Gigi, who made everything from scratch.

"That's baloney." She leans forward on the table, chin in hand. "That boy would walk across burning coals if you told him to."

I almost drop the hot pan. That wine must be stronger than she thinks. "Eli? Eli-our neighbor-Costas? No."

She puts her feet up on one of the other chairs. "Oh yes. Yes he would."

I narrow my eyes. "That's ridiculous."

"Okay, I'm sorry, I forgot," she says. "Eighteen-year-old humans know everything."

I hand her a plate with a still too-hot cinnamon roll. "Mom. Come on. Stop."

Her whole face lights up when she takes it. "Never mind, I'm not going to argue with you. Just go to the picnic. You have, what, three months left of high school? Go have some fun. If he drinks, you call his father to come and get you in a police cruiser. That'll teach him."

She laughs as I take a violent bite out of a cinnamon roll and burn my mouth.

"So you'll go? To the beach?"

I lift a shoulder, lick some icing off my fingers, and wonder why my mom thinks that Eli would do anything for me. I know he cares about me, and maybe something could have happened between us, at one time. Then I kissed him and that was the end of that.

I yank loose the strap of my bikini top. "I think this thing's too small on me now."

Mom chuckles. "No, honey, it's not too small, you've just finally filled it out."

"Mother!"

"Well I'm sorry, it's true. You, my dear, are a lovely young woman, inside and out." She picks up her glass of wine and kisses me on the forehead. "I'm going to take a shower and dive back into bed with my Scottish laird."

"Gross, Ma." She loves romance novels and has been on a Scotland kick lately. All the covers feature a very hot guy in a kilt. It's embarrassing.

My mind immediately pictures Eli in a kilt, shirtless, maybe riding a horse. Wearing his glasses. See, this is not healthy, the fantasies that I have about him, not when I've got a bona fide scientific hypothesis to prove. I shove down another cinnamon roll. I'll go to the stupid party. Only a few weeks of driving lessons, and I'll be free of him. Then my first kiss research can continue, unhindered. Maybe even at Emory.

The kitten rubs against my foot and I scoop her into my arms. "It's going to be okay, Marie. Let's go upstairs and get some scholarships."

It takes me forever to finish the applications, but I finally hit send in the early morning. I try to sleep with not much luck. Between Marie pouncing on me whenever I move and sexy dreams about kilt-wearing hotties, one hottie in particular, I get no rest.

I wake up to my phone, buzzing on the nightstand. I totally overslept. It's already ten thirty, and Eli is texting.

Mom wants to know if you want ham or turkey. I told her you don't give a shit but she made me text you.

He sticks in a growly-face emoji to make sure I know she's driving him crazy.

Ugh really don't want to go.

TEXT NOT RECEIVED

Real mature. I don't want to go.

WTF ur going. Ham or turkey?

What does he care if I go or not? I don't answer. A few minutes later:

Fine. Turk-ham it is. See you out back in thirty.

I slog out of bed and go downstairs to feed Marie. There's a note on the kitchen table next to a Sonic gift card.

Got this from a student at Xmas, only $10 but that buys a lot of slushies. Just don't add vodka, lol! Have a great time at the beach. You are my genius angel girl—it's okay to have fun!

Wow. I'm really that boring, my own mother has to tell me to have fun and jokes about alcohol?

Fine. I go upstairs, put on the freaking bikini and adjust my boobs, which aren't giant but are definitely bigger than when I wore this bikini last summer. I pull on a T-shirt and jean shorts and check myself in the mirror. My hair is pulled back. Part of me, the stubborn part, wants to leave it that way. My mother thinks I need a life? Eli thinks I need to loosen up?

No one tells me what to do. I'm fine the way I am. Marie nudges my foot.

"What, you, too?" I pull out the hair tie and let the wild mane fly. It's hot outside, though not humid, which means it actually might look halfway normal today. So I leave it down, not because I'm trying to be "fun" or to "loosen up." I leave it down because I look damn good.

I'm almost out the bedroom door when my laptop *dings*, telling me I have a new email. I open my inbox.

Thank you! Emory University has received your scholarship application.

I inhale deeply and try to push down the feeling of panic that sits just on the edge of my mind.

This is good. Everything's going according to plan. Not that there is a plan when it comes to Emory. It's more like wait and see what happens and then cross that bridge if and when I get to it. I can't control any of that scholarship business.

Truth is, I don't feel much in control of anything lately.

The only thing I can control is not drinking vodka with orange juice and washing my mind clean of Eli. I grab my keys. Time to get scrubbing.

Chapter Eight

Eli

I bring out our giant cooler that my pain-in-the-ass mom packed with enough food to feed the entire team, twice. And there's only lunch and drinks for me and Nora in there.

Nora. Who is waiting by her garage, and damn. She looks…she looks sexy. The hair doesn't help. I had this moment of clarity last night—if I really think I'm gonna make this plan work, maybe I should start treating her like a girl. Maybe compliment her. It won't be easy. It's not like I don't know how to treat a woman—I've just trained myself to ignore those things when it comes to her.

"Hey." I raise a hand. "Looking good."

Smooth, Eli. Could you just try and act normal?

Her eyes narrow. "Thanks?"

"E!" I turn and see Dad on the back porch, a scowl on his face. He has the day off so he's in his boxers and a stretched out holey T-shirt. "No drinking, you hear me?"

My brain starts to shut down. This is the start of his

drinking lecture that I've heard about a thousand times. "Yeah, Dad, I know."

He smirks. "Oh yeah? You know, do you? You know what it's like telling a parent that their kid's dead because he was driving drunk? I don't ever plan on being on the receiving end…"

…*of that call*, I finish in my head. The best thing to do is go along with it. "Yeah, Dad, I'm good. Um, pants, maybe?"

He doesn't care he's half naked in the backyard. Me, on the other hand? I care.

"Uh, hey, Nora!" Dad calls. "How are you?"

She's cringing, Dad, that's how she is.

"Good, I'm good. Thanks, Mr. Costas."

He tilts his head and squints at her. "You're going, too? To this shindig?"

Nora grunts, still in denial. "Yeah. Apparently."

Dad's head snaps to me and he points an accusing finger. "Okay then. Eli, you're driving Nora. I find out you drink, life as you know it is over."

I wish I could yell at him to leave me the hell alone. Sometimes I think he wants me to screw up and get caught. "Dad, I got it," I say, just to shut him up.

"You kids have fun, though. Just don't do anything stupid."

I inhale, trying to stay cool. I walk away, my back to him, and hear the back door shut. "Ladies and gentlemen, Police Chief Michael Costas, Dad of the year!"

She pats my back. "I love your dad so much."

I open her trunk and hoist the cooler into the back. "Oh yeah, he's adorable, unless you actually have to live with him."

"It beats having a dad you see twice a year and then it's horribly awkward because you don't even know each other," she grumbles.

"Yeah. I guess. You going to see him this summer?"

"No." Her voice gets soft. "I don't think so. He'll come for graduation. Mom and him won't talk to each other, and then he'll go home."

There she is, getting sad again. I can't let that happen, not today. "His loss," I say, not giving her any room to argue. "Let's go."

She holds out the keys for me, but I don't take them. "Your mom is at work. We don't have to switch."

The color drains from her face. I can actually hear her gulp.

Time for another pep talk. "Come on, you did great last time. This time will be even easier." I walk around to the passenger side and try to ignore the fact that my knee still hurts. I've been doing stretches, taking it easy at practice… I can't shake whatever's wrong with it, though, and I gotta stay healthy.

Nora opens the driver's side and looks at the steering wheel, terrified. She gets in anyway, backs out with the speed of a sedated tree sloth, and finally makes it to the road. Silently, slowly, she winds her way through the neighborhood. When she turns onto Main, she leans forward and peers at the sky. "I think it's gonna rain. Maybe we shouldn't go."

I rub my temple. "Okay, science genius girl, I know that there is no chance of rain, not even a little, so stop trying to con your way out of this."

Her fingers grip the steering wheel tighter. "I'm not. I just don't want to drive all the way out there if it's going to rain."

"It's not going to rain." I turn to her. She needs a distraction, so I decide this might be a good time for a compliment. "So, your hair…" I say, with no real plan for how to finish that sentence.

"What?" She touches it and glances at the rearview mirror. "Does it look bad?" She swerves into the next lane.

"Watch the road," I say. "And no. It doesn't. It doesn't

look bad at all. It looks really good," I say, but I can see in her wrinkled-up forehead that she's not buying it. My stomach churns. Maybe this isn't gonna work. Maybe I have been in her friend zone for too long.

"Thanks." She smirks. "Yours doesn't look bad, either."

This is a disaster. How can I compliment her if she doesn't believe me?

Get it together, Costas.

"Hey, you want some pie before we head out?" If she can't take a compliment, I can at least maximize our time together.

"Sure."

She pulls into the Mermaid parking lot, overshoots the turn, and scrapes the hubcap on the curb.

"Shit, shit, shit," she says. She doesn't swear much, so it sounds funny coming out of her mouth and I bust up.

"You said you wouldn't make fun of me," she says. When I look at her, though, she's not mad. In fact, there's a lopsided grin on her face. "It's true, though, I really suck." She laughs and pulls into a spot, well, half of one spot, half of another.

"See, that's what you need to do," I say. "You need to chill out; relax." I lean toward her, knowing that if this plan is going to work, I can't be afraid to get close. "And you don't suck."

She backs away, and I remind myself that this isn't going to happen overnight. We get out and I assess her parking job. "Okay, maybe you do suck. But you'll get better. I promise."

We're late to the party and I don't really care. My plan calls for us to spend time together. Which we did at the Mermaid, over underbaked chocolate cream and overbaked key lime. Nora parks in the beach lot, actually in the lines this time, and yanks out the key with confidence. "It's amazing," she says, "you didn't yell at me once."

"Don't get too cocky, we still have the drive home," I say. I'm giving her a hard time even though she did do good. She pops the trunk and I get out, breathing in the salty air. I love everything about the beach: volleyball, surfing, skimboarding, girls in bikinis... Also, there are lots of memories here, with Nora. We used to come all the time, with our families, when we were younger.

We walk side by side through the mangroves up the path to the shore, and Koviak spots us from a distance. "Hey, it's about damn time!" he yells.

"Yay," Nora says, her voice oozing sarcasm.

"Kov's a good guy," I whisper.

She huffs. "He doesn't like me."

"He likes you, Nora."

"He does not."

"Because you went out once and you dumped him? Trust me, he's over it. In fact, he thinks you're totally hot. Probably would say yes if you gave him another shot."

"Ouch!" She stops, takes off her flip-flop, and grabs my shirt sleeve for balance. She brushes off the bottom of her foot. "See, that's why I didn't want to come." I reach out a hand to steady her, holding onto her arm while she puts the flip-flop back on.

"Why?" I ask.

Her eyes rivet to mine. "Because I can't give him another shot, can I?"

"Are you asking me or telling me?"

She groans. "Eli. You know I can't. That's not the way it works."

I let go of her arm. Yeah, I do know. Better than anyone.

Suddenly I'm not in the best mood. "You know, what if you're wrong?" A group of lacrosse players passes us, grunting and shouting "Eli" like Neanderthals.

She ignores them, sets her mouth, and narrows her eyes. "What if I'm right?"

Who's gonna argue with that?

I run a hand through my hair. Me. That's who. I'm gonna prove to her she's dead wrong.

"Nora," I say. "I know you're always right and shit, but just today, why don't you try to forget all that, don't think so much, and have fun? You can do it. I know you can."

She trudges down the wooden steps to the beach. "Of course I can," she says. "I know how to have fun, Eli."

"Then prove it." I nudge her arm and smile. "It'll be a challenge, but pretend you're a normal girl."

She doesn't answer, but she starts moving again, and I figure that's answer enough.

Down on the sand, I'm instantly pulled in with a group of the guys who want to talk lacrosse. A few minutes later, I scan the crowd and I see her down near the water with Abby, who is laying out a towel next to a bunch of the other girls.

A few of them are talking to Nora. Good. Good. At least they aren't ignoring her. The most amazing thing about this scene is that they're all in bikinis, laid out on stomachs or backs. It's a beautiful sight—a sea of skin.

Thankfully, Nora is still in her shorts and T-shirt when Tex runs up to her and points to the volleyball net. Oh yeah. I'm gonna kill that guy. He's working that dopey cowboy mug of his and trying to charm her. The worst thing is, she seems to be buying it. Shit. She cannot kiss that dude.

"Volleyball, anyone?" I yell loud enough for Tex to hear. "Koviak!" I call to where he's standing next to a cooler. "Let's start a game, man!"

"Sure."

I jog over to Nora and…what's his name. "Hey." Seriously, what is his name? Something weird. "Koviak's starting a volleyball game. You should play." I thrust my thumb over my shoulder.

Another grin spreads on his big mouth. "Yeah. Sounds good." He lifts a hand to me. I'm supposed to high-five him? God, what an ass.

I leave him hanging, and he gets the hint. "You play, Nora?" he says to her.

She wrinkles up her nose. God, she's cute. "No thanks, I'll watch."

I want to do a backflip. *Denied you cow turd, now go the fuck away!*

Tex looks like someone stole his favorite lasso. "Cool, let's talk later. Maybe go for a walk?" he says, so obvious with the pickup lines I want to hurl.

Nora lifts up on her toes and, holy shit, did she just flip her hair? "Yeah. Sure. Definitely."

She has no shame.

"Aren't you gonna play?" she asks me when I don't leave with Tex to join the game.

I shake my head. "Nah, gotta protect the knee." Which is suddenly hurting like a mother. "Up for a swim?"

Her eyes do that squinty, suspicious thing. "Okay."

"Why do you always look at me like that?"

"Like what?"

I put my hands on my hips. "Like you don't believe me. I'm telling you the truth—I don't want to play. Let those jackasses ruin their knees. I want to swim. Do you want to come with me?"

She lays out her towel next to Abby's, and then she turns toward the ocean, big and powerful and infinite, lifts both arms at the same time and pulls her shirt up over her head.

Adrenaline, almost like I'm running a play, rushes through me. I mean, I guess it's adrenaline—either that, or I'm just straight up turned on. Damn. I can't look away. I haven't seen her this clothes-free in a long time. I have to concentrate on moving the air in and out of my lungs. This is Nora. This is no big deal.

Except it is.

She's wearing this little striped bikini top I can barely handle. Then she takes her shorts off next and I see the bikini bottom—same stripes, and just as small. Not a lot of coverage.

"Let's go in," she says. "I'm hot."

I run a hand through my hair. *Holy shit. You're telling me.*

Chapter Nine

NORA

Eli's acting so weird today, and I wish I knew why. Maybe he just can't believe I'm here. To be honest, neither can I.

It's a beautiful day, the sun's out, and it's hot. Not blazing hot like in the summer, but just right. Abby's here, which is good. It's nice to see a familiar face. The rest of the crew— Veronica, Aimee, Tori, and Madison—after getting over their initial shock of seeing me, act surprisingly decent.

Maybe Eli is right; maybe they don't hate me.

None of this explains him being so…attentive is the only word I can think of. The only reason I'm here is to wean myself off him, but it almost feels like he's on to my plan, and determined to thwart it.

That's ridiculous, of course. He can't read my mind.

I *do* notice he's looking at me in this bikini. Like *really* looking. Not that it matters. I've never been shy around him and I'm not going to start now. Plus, it's my body. Even though I'm not quite used to how I'm filling out this bikini top, I'm not embarrassed. My boobs—they're there. I've managed to hold only a bit of tan from last summer, and thanks to a long line of pear-shaped genetics, I got a little something going on in the back.

It's all science anyway. Nothing you can do about it, it is what it is. Might as well embrace it.

Let him look.

Plus, let's talk about him for a second. His shirt's off, and the sweat on his muscles is catching the sunlight. His tan never fades and his eyes are bright blue right now, bluer than the water in front of us. He's a Greek god, come down from Olympus to mess with us mortals. He's trying to grow out his hair—that's a lacrosse team thing, the shaggy hair. Only I know that if his gets too long it curls up like a poodle. Right now, it's perfect. The thick salty air has it sticking up in all directions. It's so sexy.

All he needs are the glasses and I'd be doomed.

What I *should* be doing is thinking of the new kid from Texas. Caleb. He's in my AP Bio class and I have yet to kiss him. He's totally handsome, tall, light-brown hair. And his body is… Let's just say, I've heard he played hockey where he came from and wow. If that's a hockey body, warm up the Zamboni and clear the ice. I mean, *wow*. He's got these high cheekbones that make him look like a comic book superhero. His lips look utterly kissable. I've checked them out. In fact, I should be playing volleyball up there with him.

Except I have zero athletic skills, and the water looks so inviting.

We walk into the surf, side by side, Eli and me. The water is chilly, but the sun is hot and it feels good. The gentle waves break on our ankles, then our knees.

Which reminds me. "How is your knee?" He's been limping and it seems to be getting worse.

He smiles. "Perfect."

He forgets how well I know him. I can hear the anxiety in his voice. As much as I don't get the appeal of lacrosse—or really any organized sport—I know he loves it.

I do wish he'd see the bigger picture, though. Back in the fall, I asked him if he was going to apply to other schools and he took major offense. *Why wouldn't we stick with our plan?* I believe is what he said. The memory fills me with dread. How am I going tell him about Emory?

Not that he could get in anywhere else. His grades suck, and his ACT score was middle of the road, but I know he could do better. He's smart, just lazy. If it's not pie or lacrosse, he's pretty much not interested.

The water laps at my bare stomach and makes me squeal. "Oh God, it's so cold!"

"Don't be such a wimp!" Eli says, splashing me.

I shiver from head to toe. "Don't!" I splash back, harder, but he doesn't care. He dives under the surface and disappears. I'm up to my chest now, and he's nowhere to be seen, and I'm tossed back in time to another day at the beach. We were maybe eleven, here with his mom, my mom, Gigi, and Ari, who wasn't even in kindergarten yet.

The water was really choppy that day, and we were fearless. We dove in and out of the waves for hours, rode them all the way in to shore.

Then, all of a sudden, he was gone.

He'd gotten pulled under and didn't come back up. Even then, I knew about science, about tides, and the ocean and how it worked. I knew about riptides, and how to swim out of them and not drown. Eli had no idea.

Our moms and Gigi came running into the water, all of them screaming his name. Without even thinking, I dove under, my small hands searching for Eli. Truth was, there was no way I was coming up without him.

Finally I found him, or his leg anyway, and I clamped

onto him and pulled him to me. It was like I had superhuman strength. His mom got him to shore and he spit out water and I gave him the biggest hug and cried my eyes out.

To this day I've never been more scared in my life.

He pops up again and I'm back in the present. He's right in front of me. Closer than he probably should be. I try to step backward, but the tide is not having it.

He pushes his hair back, and his wet skin glistens. "Where are you?"

I should try to step back again. He's so close. "What do you mean? I'm right here."

"Are you? You look really far away."

My stomach flutters. I'm nervous. I glance toward shore where I should be, with Caleb who I have not kissed. I don't see him anywhere. I don't see anything with Eli right in front of me.

"Remember that time you got pulled under?" I ask.

Is he moving closer to me? I can almost feel the warm sun reflecting off him.

He cocks his head and the dimple comes out. I'm wobbly on my legs. "I remember. You saved my life."

Why is he so close?

"Did I ever thank you for that?"

I don't know what to do right now except try to act normal. "You totally acted like it was no big deal, like you had it all under control. Then you threw up salt water for two hours."

Did he just move closer again? Or is it me, moving closer to him?

He laughs, soft but deep, a man's laugh. A *good* laugh—kind, not sarcastic or teasing. "In my defense, I was a little shit."

We've moved into deeper water; my toes are barely grazing the sandy bottom now. I lose my footing and start to tread water. He's not backing away. I know I should back off, except I can't. There's something holding me here and it feels good. "You were, sometimes, yes," I say. "You usually made up for it. Like, I remember when we got home you helped Gigi bake a pie, and you gave it to me. You would have never admitted it to my face, but I knew that was a thank-you."

"Oh, right. Cranberry apple." He raises a brow. "You know how hard it is to find cranberries in the summer?" Under the surface, his hands touch mine.

I jerk away. "What are you doing?" I ask, suddenly terrified. This is the opposite of what should be happening.

He laughs again. "Jesus. Relax. I'm trying to keep you from sinking. Just hold on to my shoulders." He lifts both of my hands to rest just above his clavicles. His skin is warm.

There are parts of my body growing warm, too.

I shouldn't keep my hands here, I tell myself. I should move them immediately, but there's nothing I can do to stop this. Those eyes have become tractor beams in a sci-fi movie. I'm caught in them, powerless to escape.

"Where did you find them?" I'm doing everything I can to make this seem normal, even though none of this is normal.

"Find what?" He lifts his hands out of the water and grips my forearms. He's got to put them somewhere, right?

I swallow hard. "The cranberries?"

"Oh. Gigi knew a guy. Had some in his freezer."

Yes, let's talk about Gigi, that should cool me down. "You used to make pies with her all the time. I wish you hadn't stopped. You could be making us good pie."

His forehead creases up. "Yeah, it was always fun hanging out with her, then I got busy, I guess. Plus, you know, pie baker doesn't really fit the image."

I smirk. "Oh God. What image is that?"

He grins. "You know. Stud. Lacrosse beast. Superfly dude."

I groan. "Oh no, is that what you've been going for?"

A corner of his mouth lifts. "Not pulling it off?"

Unable to stop myself, I lift my hand off his shoulder, poke his dimple lightly, then put my hand right back where it was. "Oh, Eli," I say. "You can't fool me. I know who you are."

His hands move higher upon my arms and a silence floats between us.

His mouth twitches. "Who am I?"

My friend. Friend. *Friend.*

"Who do you want to be?"

What the hell am I saying?! I must be possessed.

His eyebrows pull together, and I am aware that I'm looking at his mouth. At those full, gorgeous lips. I'm also aware that I want to…kiss them.

But then there's splashing, and his teammates are tumbling toward us like prehistoric ape-men, shouting and tearing up the smooth surface around us, and the moment is lost.

That's okay, because the moment needed to be lost.

I let go of Eli as the guys descend. He says nothing when I turn back to shore and leave.

Back on the beach, Abby offers me a water bottle. "Hey, you went in?" She didn't notice us out there and I'm glad. She chatters on and on about how hot they all look, the lacrosse guys out there. I barely hear her, because my heart is pumping so hard, scared by what just happened, by what almost happened.

My mind races in time with my pulse. I sit cross-legged on the towel and remind myself of my hypothesis. I go over the story of Gigi and Harold. Eli is not mine. Even if I almost kissed him out there.

I can't do that. Can. Not. No matter how badly I wanted to, that's not how this theory works.

Chapter Ten

Eli

"Clear the crease! Clear the crease!" I shout at the top of my lungs. It's almost all rookies out there on the field—most of them juniors, except for Tex.

Koviak jumps up and down next to me. "These assholes can't play!"

He's right.

"Fucking Tex is the only one out there who has any game," he complains. "We're so screwed!"

"All right, keep it down." Some of these players come from select clubs, and some of them I've played with. They have skills, but not if they think we don't believe in them. The game is like that, which Koviak knows well. You get too much in your own head and you might as well give up.

It's Saturday, we have a tough game on Tuesday, and some of us are still hurting from the beach party yesterday, including Koviak, who somehow managed to sneak in a cooler full of "fruit punch" bottles that he'd spent way too much time spiking with whatever booze he'd managed to scrounge up. Dude's pretty resourceful when he wants to be.

Of course, I didn't have a drop, thanks to Nora Reid and my boxer-shorts-wearing cop father. Not that I'm an alcoholic or anything, but it sure would've taken the edge off of yesterday—and there was an edge, at least from my view. Out there in the water, I was doing my thing, working my plan, and I almost kissed her. I wanted to so badly, and my body started to respond accordingly, and I didn't know what to do.

I've never been so glad to have a bunch of assholes interrupt my alone time with a pretty girl. And damn, yesterday, that's what she was. Not just Nora—she was someone else.

I didn't let that scare me off, though. In fact, after that I was probably in her face too much, trying to keep Tex out of it. Caleb, that's his name. What kind of name is that? Dumbass stupid Texas cowboy name.

Now, back in the locker room, I've cranked "You Can Call Me Al," an old Paul Simon song that my dad loves, on the sound system. I've picked it to be this year's team song. It's one of my jobs as captain.

"Yo, Highlanders!" I call to the mass of my sweaty, near-dead and hungover teammates. "Listen to this song. This is *the* song, brothers. You hear this song, and you remember that 'you ain't soft in the middle, you ain't got a short little span of attention.'" They stare at me like I'm crazy as I quote the weird lyrics. "'When you want a photo opportunity—you need a shot at redemption. Not gonna end up a cartoon in a cartoon graveyard!' You hear this song, and you remember that together we're unbeatable—that we have each other's backs, that we are the Highlanders, and *this* is our season!"

The whole team erupts like a volcano, waving shafts and helmets in the air, and I crank the music up while they dance around like idiots.

When it ends, Koviak nudges me as I head to my locker. "Weird song. But catchy."

"It's no 'Dancing Queen.'" I say, remembering the seniors from last year who picked that song. It was stupid, too, and it caught on. Whenever the team song plays, no matter what the climate of the practice, or the game, it puts a smile on everyone's face and reminds us why we do this—to have fun and kick ass.

"So..." Koviak nudges me. "You have a good time yesterday?"

I sit on the bench between the lockers, thinking. "Yeah." Though Nora couldn't wait to get away from me in that water. Then afterward, she acted totally normal, like nothing happened. None of that was good.

His eyes bore into my skull. "You're into her again, aren't you?"

"Why? You gonna give me some love advice?"

He screws up his mouth and lifts a shoulder. "You want some?"

"No!" I slam my locker shut, towel wrapped around my waist. "Dude, you know we go way back. She's just a friend."

He sniffs. "Didn't look like just friends to me. Out there in the water, the two of you."

"Oh yeah, and what exactly does *just friends* look like, as if you've ever been just friends with a female?"

He inclines his head toward me. "Just friends means you don't look like you're about to make out."

My jaw tenses. "I gotta hit the showers."

"Fine, fine, go take your cold shower. Just be aware, Tex is most definitely on the move."

I don't look back at Kov as I walk away, and when I pass Tex at his locker, I have to once again check every impulse to slam him into the lockers.

I shower off quick and work out my next step with Nora. If Koviak is right—and he knows everything—Tex might ask her out. I don't have time to waste.

I don't want to say I've become obsessed with this challenge, but yeah, okay, I'll say it. I'm going to prove this hypothesis wrong. What will it take? I'm sure as hell gonna find out.

I get back to my locker, and it's like a lightbulb flips on in my head. Pie. The one thing that fixes everything.

Out in Michael Jordan, I take a minute to Google the place I'm thinking of, then I text her.

You busy?

Why?

Time for another lesson.

By the time I get home, she hasn't responded, so I get out of the truck and head for her back door. Her mom opens it before I can knock.

"Eli! I haven't seen you in forever. Come on in!"

"Hey, Ms. Reid. Is Nora home?" I go inside the kitchen, where the wall is burned up above the oven. I know she's worried about the money, but she needs to get that fixed.

"Nora!" she yells out into the depths of the house. Their house is old, probably over a hundred years, and Gigi lived in it forever. I think of all the time I spent in the kitchen with her before Nora even moved here. When Ari was little and Mom and Dad were taking him from doctor to doctor, trying to figure out what was wrong, trying to get him the help he needed, Gigi's is where I went. We had some good times in here, and made some awesome pies.

Nora slides into the kitchen in her socks, a tank top, and short shorts. I have to look away again. What's with me?

"Yes?" When she sees me, her mouth drops open a little. "Oh, hey, what's up?"

"Did you get my text?"

She's thinking of a reason to say no. "Oh, um yeah, except I have to…"

Don't even try it. I'm not taking no for an answer. "You ready to head out?"

"Where you going?" Ms. Reid asks.

I flash her the Costas dimple. Even she can't fight it. "I need to run an errand for my mom." Which isn't even a total lie—she asked me to pick up dessert for her book club meeting. "Up the coast a little. MJ's been giving me a little trouble, so I thought we could take Nora's car. If that's okay?"

Ms. Reid bites her bottom lip, just like her daughter does. "Okay. Just be careful. My ex supposedly has it insured, so he says…"

Nora crosses her arms, looks at the floor. She doesn't like it when her mom trash talks her dad, even if it's all true.

"No, I'll be careful. Don't worry." *So will your kid, who will be doing the actual driving.*

I don't like lying to her. She's a good person, Ms. Reid, but I have to stick to the plan. Nora still hasn't said a word to her about the driving, or Emory either, I'm guessing. I'd be an idiot if I didn't take advantage of that. I can totally blackmail the hell out of her. "I'll meet you outside, Nor."

Just like that, I'm out the back door. I'm not going to stop my plan now, even if it did get weird yesterday. It's time for the full-court press.

She'll thank me when I prove her theory wrong.

Chapter Eleven

NORA

"Merge! Now! Merge!"

Eli is yelling as I try to get onto the highway. Doesn't he know that a stressed-out driver is a dangerous driver?

My nerves are frayed, and I swallow hard. "Don't yell at me!" Finally I merge and almost clip a semi.

We're in heavy traffic and I don't like it at all. It's possible that I'm not getting enough oxygen. *Breathe, Nora, breathe.*

"Good job," he says, but his voice is shaky. "That was good."

I don't respond, too busy keeping an eagle eye on the car in front of me, ignoring the fact that giant trucks have me penned in on both sides. "What exit is it?" I screech.

"Four miles. Only four miles. You got this. You're doing good, you could pass the test tomorrow."

That can't be true. "Don't lie to me."

"I mean it, your focus is there," he says. "Focus is key. And you're going over the speed limit, that's progress."

He's a liar, but I bite my bottom lip and push through the fear. Hitting the driver's ed instructor was a careless accident that isn't going to happen again. Driving is not that big a deal, everyone does it. Just like everyone leaves home, or falls in love.

The difference between me and everyone else—I like to get things right the first time. I'm a control freak. I realize we can't know our futures, so if I can make an educated guess in order to ensure my happiness, why wouldn't I?

Eli sighs loudly, probably because I'm going fifty miles per hour in a sixty-five mile per hour."

Case in point. When it comes to him, kissing him…it was a bad outcome. I need to get over it and keep searching for a good outcome. That's all.

He points to a giant green highway sign. "That's you. Two miles."

I glance his way, so glad he can't read my mind. "Where are we going anyway? What does your mother need all the way out here?"

"Something for her book club."

"Like what?"

"You'll see. Turn signal. Here."

I veer onto the exit, hopeful that I can get out of this car soon.

"See?" he continues. "That wasn't so bad. Rush hour is easy."

I come to the stop sign at the end of the exit ramp and the car behind me honks for some unknown reason. "What?" I shout back over my shoulder. "Go away, I hate you!"

Eli laughs. "Don't worry, they'll stop honking eventually. It'll all be worth it." He points into the distance when the light turns green. "Go right."

I do as he says. "It better be."

He motions to a restaurant on the corner. "Okay, right

there."

The sign says TICK TOCK DINER. "What's that?" I ask.

"Just a little place that turned up when I Googled 'Best pie in Florida.' I was gonna save it for another time, but you needed another lesson, and I was hungry."

I have to admit, I'm excited. The "Best pie in Florida" sounds perfect after that drive. I pull into the parking lot, manage to park mostly between two lines, and turn off the engine. One look at him and I see the dimple. I think of touching it yesterday in the water. I shouldn't have done that.

Of course, I'm not going to bring up what happened yesterday. I'm pretty sure it was all my imagination anyway. It was hot out, I might have been dehydrated. There's no way he wanted to kiss me. We're just way too comfortable with each other. He might have been into me back in eighth grade, but he's not now. To think otherwise is just me being stupid. He knows my hypothesis. He knows I take it seriously, even if he thinks it's a joke.

Inside the restaurant it's like stepping back in time. There's a big clock with a lit-up face that says TICK TOCK DINER SINCE 1949 hanging behind the cash register. It's bright and the light gives everything a vintage glow, like an old sepia-toned picture. It's cozy in here, like home.

Eli looks for someone to seat us, and I am drawn to the baked goods case like a moth to a bug light.

I gaze longingly at the lineup of pies. "What is this madness?" I whisper reverently when Eli joins me.

An old woman in a waitress uniform shuffles over. "Just take a seat wherever you want, kids." We thank her but stick around a few minutes longer to drool over the case.

"Check out that one," I say. "Black bottom pie? God. And that one." I smack him in the arm. "Eli. Triple berry lemon. Triple. Berry. Lemon!"

"I told you. Best pie in Florida. Let's sit down." He steps

aside to let me pass and I feel his hand, lightly, on the small of my back. Or maybe I imagined that, too.

Fran is the name embroidered on the white-haired waitress's uniform. She sets down two glasses of ice water and offers us a half smile. "You kids want dinner? We got a beef stew special tonight. Real good. Free slice of pie if you have room for it after."

"Oh, we'll have room," Eli says, arching his eyebrows at me. "You want dinner?" he asks. "My treat."

I frown. He never pays for anything. We always split checks because that's what friends do. "No, I have money."

He smirks. "This isn't a male dominance thing. I want to pay, okay?"

Fran huffs.

I glare at him. "Why?"

He leans back against the booth and tilts his head. "Because I want to. And stop looking at me like that."

I glance sideways at Fran, who seems to be enjoying this.

"All right, we settled then?" she asks. "Gentleman pays. Nothing wrong with that on a date."

"No," I quickly add. "We're just friends."

"All righty then. Just friends. Got it. What would you like?"

I sit up taller, unsure of what's happening here. "I'll have the special, and a slice of triple berry lemon, please." My tone is curt, because this is not a date. I'm sure she's a nice lady, but Fran seems awfully up in our business.

"What can I get for you, big spender?" she asks.

He looks over the menu, not focusing on anything. "I'll have the special, too. With a Coke, and a slice of the black bottom pie. Please."

Fran nods her head. "Good choice. That's my favorite. Been our specialty since the place opened."

I hand her my menu and Eli does the same, except she

winks at him.

As she walks away, I make an observation. "God. The ladies can't resist you, Costas, young or old."

He winks at me. "What can I say? It's a curse." He beats a quick rhythm on the tabletop. "So—what do you think?"

"Of this place? I think this is what heaven is like." I sit back on the green vinyl booth bench. Maybe it's just me, but this sort of *does* feel like a date.

I inhale deep. This is not going according to plan. If I'm going to kill this crush, I have to go for the jugular. I don't want to—I *have* to. "So, plans tonight? Big date?" I hold my breath waiting for his reply.

"Nope." He hits me again with the dimple. It's like a tranquilizer gun and I'm an elephant he's trying to bring down. "I'm keeping my options open. You never know what can happen."

That's my cue. "Well"—I level my gaze at him—"you *can* know. If you take a scientific approach."

He laughs. "Oh, right," he says in a nerdy professor voice. "The scientific approach. I can find true love as long as I'm willing to collect and analyze data."

I glare at him, more than a little annoyed. "You know, sometimes I wish I never told you about my theory. I should have just let you think I was a bitch. Left it at that."

His eyes get wide when I use that word. He knows I hate it.

Fran reappears with Eli's Coke. He sticks in the straw and takes a drag and I'm reminded of that garage kiss, all those years ago.

He plays with the straw wrapper, twisting it into nothing. "Sometimes I wish you hadn't told me, either. I probably could have gotten over you easier if I thought you rejected me because I was ugly, or had too many zits, or was a dork."

He finally looks up and his eyes burn me like lasers.

"Knowing it was just that one lousy kiss made it impossible."

Impossible to what? Get over me? Does that mean he's *not* over me?

Fran emerges from the back with a tray. "Here we go, kids."

I lose the staring contest, breaking my gaze first. I must have heard him wrong. She places big white bowls in front of us, filled with meat, carrots, and potatoes in a thick brown gravy.

"Thank you," I say quietly.

"I'll give you some time to eat, then bring out your pie." She walks away and an odd silence lingers between us.

He clears his throat. "I'm just saying, Nora. Have you ever wondered, if you tried to kiss me again now, if it would be different?"

"Eli. It doesn't work that way."

"Right." He picks up his fork.

He's making my brain hurt, and I'm losing control. I need to change the subject—now—and I can't think of a thing to say. Finally, he swallows a mouthful of food and speaks. "It's okay, though. No worries. You have your theories." He takes a sip of his Coke. "I have mine."

"*You* do?"

His jaw drops in mock outrage. "What, you think I can't come up with a hypothesis?"

My palms are sweaty. Something about this is making me very uneasy, but I have to act normal. "No, of course you can. Care to share?"

"I don't know." He takes another bite of stew. "I'm not sure you can handle it."

"All right. I'll take that dare. Try me."

"Okay." He waves his fork in the air. "My theory is that your theory is totally bogus, which of course, you already know. What you don't know is *why* it's bogus…"

He pauses like he's going for some sort of dramatic effect. "Chaos theory."

I choke on my food, take a sip of water, and try not to laugh. "Chaos theory?"

His dimple digs deeper. "Yes. Exactly. Do you even know what it is?"

Clearly he's been waiting to use this. I narrow my eyes. "Yes, a little."

"Good, so I won't bore you with the basics. See, you"—he points his fork at me—"think love is predictable. Like gravity and electricity or chemical equations. All that shit. While I"—he points the fork at himself—"I believe it's unpredictable. Like the weather and the stock market."

"The stock market?"

He shrugs. "Yeah. I mean, why not?"

I smile, just a little, at the thought of proving him wrong. "Except the stock market can be predicted, somewhat, and so can the weather. There are signs, benchmarks that scientists and analysts know to look for."

He smiles, too. "Okay, but say a weather dude predicts that there's going to be a hurricane, and that it's gonna hit Edinburgh."

"You mean a meteorologist?"

"Yeah, sure, whatever." He waves that fork around like a wild man. "So he predicts it's gonna hit us head on, and then this weird little storm pops up off the coast of Africa." He stops. "You still following?"

I cross my arms. "Yes, Eli."

"Good. So this storm pops up and makes ripple effects that change the course of our hurricane and it ends up turning north in the Atlantic and not hitting a damn thing." He finally puts his fork down. "That's called the butterfly effect."

I press my lips together. "Eli?"

"Nora?"

"Have you been reading Wikipedia again?"

He chuckles and takes another bite. "Doesn't matter where I read it. It makes sense to me."

He's tried to make me doubt my theory before, but I'm not so easily convinced. "Look, I respect your theory, but I think you're wrong. You forget I have proof. Gigi and Harold knew it when it happened because they paid attention to the signs, followed through, and had a beautiful life together."

The fork starts to wave again. "Yeah, maybe, but it wasn't perfect. Didn't he die pretty young? Not perfect. And now Gigi almost burns their house down and has to live in an old folks home? Not perfect at all."

I stab a piece of beef. "I'm not saying their life was perfect. I'm saying the life they had together, the love they shared—was."

He twists up his mouth. "You *know* that?"

I tell myself to stay calm. *You're a scientist. Act like one. Scientists are challenged all the time. You can't take it personally.* "She told me the story my whole life."

"Yeah," he says. "She told me, too. It's a good story, but it's not the whole story."

He's starting to piss me off. "What's your point, Eli?"

He sits up taller. "What if she'd met Harold earlier? What if she kissed him when he was thirteen, and had a mouth full of braces, and had just drank half a Coke and had to burp real bad? If there had been nothing to that first kiss, and she'd moved on, you wouldn't be here." Another point of the fork and a know-it-all grin. "The butterfly effect."

"But it *didn't* happen that way. They found each other, and that's how it's going to happen for me. And would you stop pointing that fork at me?"

I push away my bowl. I don't want to talk about this anymore.

He's still smiling, like he knows he's gotten under my skin and he's enjoying it. He points his fork at me again, then at my bowl. "You gonna eat that?"

I cross my arms. "No."

He pulls my stew to his side of the booth and I wonder why it's not easier to stop liking him. He obviously enjoys messing with me and knows absolutely nothing about scientific method. A kiss *with* chemistry is different from a kiss without chemistry. Period. Butterfly effect, my ass.

Chapter Twelve

Eli

I'm getting to her. I can tell. Either that or I'm just pissing her off. It's a fine line. "Look, I'm just trying to explain how I feel. I know you have your ideas, and that's fine, but I have mine, too. Capisce?"

She inhales deep and purses those kissable lips. "Capisce."

Luckily, Fran shows up just in time to break the tension. Tension that I created. I was trying to make a point, even though I only spent like ten minutes reading about chaos theory on Wikipedia, just long enough to form a bullshit hypothesis of my own. The weird thing is, I think I made sense. Of course, she won't acknowledge that. She just sits there, looking angry.

"All right you two. Time for pie?" Fran asks.

"Can't wait," I say.

She walks away and Nora stays silent.

"Come on," I say. "Don't be mad. I want you to be happy, Nora. I want you to fall in love and be happy forever." I take a sip of Coke. *Push, Costas, push.* "I do sometimes get tired of watching you kiss all these losers, and being the biggest loser on your list."

Her angry face crumbles. Bull's-eye. "You're not a loser, Eli. God."

Fran brings the pie, gives each of us our slice, and everything else gets forgotten.

Nora digs in first. It's hard not to watch her—like with most things she's got a method. She sticks her fork in the pie, swoops it up in an arc toward her mouth. She studies it closely. This must be a scientist thing because I would have eaten the whole slice by now. The fork slips into her mouth, her lips close around it, her eyes close, and she smiles.

"This is literally the best thing I've ever eaten," she says about her triple berry lemon. She swallows, takes a sip of water, then reaches over and takes a forkful of mine. She doesn't ask. She doesn't have to.

"Oh, that's not right," she says of my pie. "That's unbelievable."

"I better try some before you eat it all." I do try it and holy shit, it's good. "What is *in* this?"

"I have no idea." She dives in for another forkful. "Screw my hypothesis, I'm in love with this pie."

Hmm. I guess that's better than Tex.

We eat all of it, practically licking the plates, and our conversation magically turns back to normal things. Friend things.

As I listen to her talking about how the cat attacked her foot the other night while she slept, I think maybe she's starting to crack. It's just a hairline fracture, but I knew this wasn't going to be easy. The important thing is, I've made some progress.

At least I think I have until her phone lights up on the table, and I can't help but see the screen. It's a text. From

Caleb.

I pretend not to notice because it's none of my business, but something's happening to me. My pulse pumps faster, and my face feels hot. All I know is this—I don't want her to kiss him. Not now, not ever. She just…can't. But short of putting that motherfucker in a box and shipping him back to Texas, I have no other choice.

It's time to double down.

•••

By the end of the week I know for a fact that nothing's happened between them. There's been no time. Nora's been staying late for the state Science Olympiad practice and she's getting rides home with Abby or her mom. I've been taking her to school in the morning, but we don't talk much at 6:50 a.m. We never have, it's just too damn early.

Evening practice has been running long and Coach has been working us hard. The good thing is, Tex is always there. It makes me feel a little better, being able to keep my eye on him. I just wish we had time for more lessons.

I don't have time to waste. I watch him watching her in the cafeteria, in the halls. He stops her whenever she walks by, and says something that makes her laugh. Makes me crazy. I wish he wasn't turning out to be such a good player so I could actually hate him.

Friday night practice is always a killer, but this one will be brutal. We've only won two of our first four games and we are not losing on Tuesday. My future coach from Citrus State will be there, and possibly scouts from other schools. All the guys are on edge. Not Tex. Maybe it's because this is his first year playing. Maybe hockey players don't think like we do. Maybe it's because he doesn't want to play in college, if he's even going.

Before we head out to the field, I pass him in the locker room. He's goofing off with a few of the rookies who've been playing like shit.

"Hey." I push his shoulder, hard enough for him to feel it under his pads.

"Yeah?" He's got these dumbass cow eyes. "What's up, Cap?"

Cap? This guy can't be serious, and he's not that smart if he hasn't picked up on the fact I don't like him.

"Yeah, just so you know, 'cause I don't know if anyone has told you, but Tuesday's a big game. Now's not the time to be screwing around." I glare at the rest of them. "Any of you. You might not give a shit about looking good to colleges, but I do. A lot of us do. If you're not gonna take it serious, you can all go back down to JV, or back to your clubs. I don't really care. I don't want you on the team if you're not giving us everything."

Wow. I sound like an intimidating prick, and Tex and the rookies are appropriately respectful, which they better be.

"Now go. Get out there."

They run ahead, out of the locker room to the field, but Tex lags behind and waits for me. "Hey, Eli," he says with that annoying as hell twang, "I want you to know I'm dead serious about this team, and about the game Tuesday. It's looking more and more like I'm gonna play in college, so I do want to impress the coaches. Me and the guys, we were just blowing off steam back there."

I've never been so tempted to stick my shaft out and trip someone. I'd save a body check for him if Coach wouldn't make me pay for it. That'll only happen if it looks like I did it on purpose, though, and I'm not bad at making my hits look like accidents when the situation calls for it.

"Yeah, good," I say through gritted teeth.

"All right. See you out there." He runs ahead.

Yeah, you will.

We warm up, do some drills, and then Coach has us run some plays. I pull off my pinnie, flip it inside out, and put it back on. I'm on the same team as Koviak and a few of the other seniors. Unfortunately we've also got a few of the more squirrelly rookies, and just my luck, we're stuck with Tex. There goes the bruise I'd planned for him.

I get the ball in the face-off, easily scooping it away from Justin Tidwell, who I've been playing with forever. He's way too easy to read. We're running a Duke so I set up a pick to Koviak who is behind the cage. The idea is he'll dodge off to his right and the midfielder, who in this play is Tex, will get the pick from Koviak in the crease and he'll be able to score.

Sam is goalie, though, and Ed and Mike Ponti are d-poles with a mission to kill. They're playing with everything they've got. It's good to see, until Tex is denied, which pisses me off.

As for me, I'm playing my ass off, but my knee still feels stiff, and I know I'm favoring my good leg. Which means I don't move as fast, or as smooth as usual.

"Costas!" Coach calls, waving me over. "Your knee okay?"

"Coach, I'm good." Nothing is wrong with my knee. It's better than it was. My surgery was two years ago. It's totally healed, and strong. I've been doing my stretches and extra leg curls to ensure that. The joints can get stiff for lots of different reasons, and most of them wouldn't require me stepping out of the game. I just have to stop babying it and play.

"Well then play like you're good."

"Yeah, yeah, I will. Sorry, Coach."

"Get back out there and run that again. This time let Gray take the face-off. See if that hockey did him any good."

Coach waves me away, and I head back out to the field, my gut burning with anger. Gray is Caleb Gray.

"Gray!" I shout to Tex. "Coach wants you on face-off."

Saying the words just pisses me off more, and when he gets the ball, I'm ready, in position. When I see one of the rookies dicking around when he's supposed to be in the crease, I break the play and run where he should be.

"Gray!" I yell, to get his attention. I've got a d-pole riding me, but if he can get me the ball, I'm gonna score. The ball goes airborne, and I set up to get the pick. It lands like a bird in my net. Then I pivot to line up the shot, and when I do...

POP.

I drop like a sack of potatoes. Fuuuuucccck. It's my knee, and not my bad knee, it's the other one. I roll on the ground, pain searing through my whole body. I know exactly what's happened. I'm rolling on my back. Coach and Mack, our trainer, run over. I'm aware of the team around me, I just can't make sense of what they're saying. The sky above me is filled with flashing lights. I close my eyes and the lights go out—on my senior season, and maybe even a college career. My whole damn life goes dark.

I passed out, but not for long. Coach and Mack stand over me and I tell them exactly what I felt. I know what happened. We all know what happened.

They get me to the locker room. The guys hover. I know they're worried, I get it. I just want them all to go away, though, to leave me alone in this locker room. I haven't cried in maybe ten years. Right now, it's all I can do to keep myself from totally wailing like a baby.

"Let's get you in the office," Mack says. There's a couch in there and my knee goes up. He brings ice packs while Coach makes the call home. He hangs up, leans against the desk, and crosses his arms.

"I know what you're thinking, Costas," he says.

My whole body is on fire right now, between the pain in my knee and the pain of knowing I'm done. I can't even look at him.

"This isn't the end, kid. You had four good games, and a great season last year. Plus, no matter what, we still need you this season. You're the captain. These guys look up to you. As soon as you do what you gotta do to fix that knee, I expect you back on the sidelines, you hear me?"

I nod once, pissed that there's actually a tear dripping down my cheek.

"Your folks are on the way, kid. I'm gonna give you a few minutes." He grips my shoulder as he passes by and closes the door behind him.

I grit my teeth and wipe my face. No way am I gonna break down. I can't. Even if this whole year has gone to shit. Nora and Emory University. No idea what I'm gonna do with my life. Now this.

I'm cursed.

The door opens, and Koviak sticks his head inside. "Hey, dickweed."

"Fuck off."

He closes the door behind him and sits on the edge of the desk.

My chest muscles constrict. I gotta keep myself together. I'm not gonna cry, even though Kov looks like he might. He knows how bad this is. Coach can try to keep my spirits up all he wants, but this might be the end. We both know it.

"Dude," he says and runs a hand through his hair. "Just get that goddamn knee fixed so you can kick ass at State next year."

I huff. "Yeah like that's still gonna happen."

"What are you talkin' about? You came back before. You'll come back from this. If they cut you, someone better will get you. Fuck 'em." He stands up, sticks out his fist for me to bump like a lame ass. "You know what else, Costas? It's just a game. Get your knee fixed. Graduate. Make your move with Reid."

I sneer. "What are you talking about?"

"You know what I'm talking about. Tex is driving, man. Time to play some D."

I suck in air, swallow down the throbbing pain in my leg. "You don't know what you're talking about."

"I know you got some free time now. Keep your eye on the prize. Get the girl."

I shift on the couch and flinch. My knee fucking hurts. "You better go," I say. "They need someone out there who knows how to play. And thanks, man."

Koviak takes off and I stare at the ceiling and imagine Nora here, now. She'd sit, maybe hold my hand, probably lecture me on how lacrosse puts joints under too much stress. Maybe she'd lean over me, watch me with those eyes. Maybe she'd kiss me.

Or, more likely, like me staying healthy, or me getting into a decent college, or me having skills in anything worth anything—it's never gonna happen.

Maybe I should just face reality. I'm going nowhere.

Chapter Thirteen

It's Friday night and everything is wrong. Mr. and Mrs. Costas are with Eli at the ER, and Ari is with me. Mom's still not home from class, and I invited Abby over to hang out, in an attempt to expand my social life.

She's grounded, but her parents let her come anyway.

"Thanks for getting me out of the house." She pushes through the kitchen, arms laden with Chinese takeout, into the dining room. "Five months until I leave for Miami. I might not survive."

She's majoring in biochemistry and molecular biology at the University of Miami. I'm not sure if she got any scholarships, but her dad is a dentist and her mom was a child TV star, so I don't think money is really an issue.

"Why'd they let you out?" I ask.

"Oh, because it's you. My mom thinks you're perfect. She totally trusts you."

I stop and stare at her. It's been years since I've even seen her mom. "Why?"

"Because you never do anything wrong?"

I grab some paper plates from the pantry. "Doesn't she remember the vodka incident of sophomore year?"

Abby groans. "That was eons ago. And I know deep down she thinks it was all me."

I screw up my mouth—she thinks I'm a total nerd. "I remember it being a pretty mutual decision." I guess I'm the only one who learned a lesson.

Ari joins us in dining room, Marie trailing after him. "Have you met Ari?" I ask her.

"You're Eli's brother? Hey. You want an eggroll?" she asks him.

"Yes," he says and sits.

"Do you want me to get rid of Marie?" I ask him. She can get annoying, especially at meal times.

His eyes snap to mine. "No!" I know he's anxious. He knows something's wrong with Eli. He takes a bite of eggroll. "Eli's dying," he says with his mouth full.

I reach out to him, careful not to touch. "He's not dying, Ari. He hurt his knee, but he's going to be fine. He'll be back home with your mom and dad soon, I promise."

He doesn't look convinced.

"Here, hold on a second."

I have an idea to FaceTime Eli and have him talk to his brother. I text first to make sure he's available. I don't want to get Ari's hopes up. Eli doesn't even respond to the text before my screen starts ringing in with a call. I answer and there's Eli, staring up at me.

My heart involuntarily flutters when I see him. "Hey!" I say.

"Damn, you're a sight for sore eyes."

Um, what? "Okay... Hey, Ari's here. Can you talk to him?"

"Yeah, put him on!"

I give the phone to Ari, who lights up when he sees his brother's face. "Hey my man, what's up?" Eli asks. Ari proceeds to interrogate him about where he is, what he's doing, and when exactly he'll be home. Eli knows just what to say to ease his mind.

"Okay, dude, I gotta go get an x-ray, but I'll be home soon. Give me back to Nora, all right?"

Ari nods and hands me the phone.

"Hey." He's grinning. "How you doin'?"

I focus on his dimple and not on the fact that he's in the hospital, hurt. "I'm fine. Are you okay?"

"I'm good. Not feeling a thing. What are you doing?"

Great. He wants to chat. He's totally high right now. "Just hanging out with Abby and Ari," I say.

He giggles like a little kid, for a solid thirty seconds.

"Eli?"

"Okay. All right. Good. Just stay away from Tex."

"What?"

"No, no, don't worry. I'm not ordering you around. I'm not gonna tell Nora Reid what to do." He's giggling again. "He's just not right for you."

This conversation is getting weird. "Okay. I should go, Eli."

"Okay?" He turns to someone offscreen. "Okay gotta go. Bye."

"Oh my God," Abby says and takes a bite of her lo mein.

I puff out a breath. "What?"

She swallows. "He totally wants you."

I'm very aware of Ari, still busy eating his eggroll. I lower my voice. "No, he doesn't. We're friends. And he's on drugs."

A corner of her mouth turns up. "Girl, what we say on painkillers? That's what we mean."

I push around my fried rice with my fork. "No. We're

friends. He's my ride, that's the only reason we hang out so much. He's my driver and only for a little while longer."

She chuckles "Oh yeah? Why's that?"

"I'm getting my license. The Friday before spring break." It's true. I made the appointment after that bizarre conversation at the Tick Tock that scared me into action. I need to stop hanging out with him so much because the crush is *not* lessening. If anything, it's getting worse. For the good of science, I need to get my license.

Abby's eyes get wide—terror, that's what I see.

"You're getting your license?"

Translation: *you broke that poor woman's leg, and now you want to drive?*

This is one con about living in a small town. Everyone knows your business, everyone is familiar with the skeletons in your closet. Especially the ones with broken femurs.

"Yes, I am." Times like these I think it might be better to leave. "Don't worry. It's been two years, and it was an *accident*. I know how to drive."

Her face relaxes. "If you say so." She takes another bite of food. "You know, you should ask him to the prom."

I glance at Ari, who is humming now and finishing his eggroll.

Teeth clenched, I glare at her. "No," I say. "You're not listening to me, Abby."

Her gaze meets mine. "Why, because he's in the friend zone? *Pfft!* Girl, you're in control of your own friend zone. Get in there and yank his ass out. He's totally into you."

I push away my plate while Ari still hums. "Why don't we watch a movie?" I suggest, desperate to get off the subject of Eli—and me.

"Someone's in denial," Abby sings.

"I'm not in denial." What I am is beginning to wish I hadn't invited her over.

She points at me and almost chokes on her fried rice. "Yeah you are. Look at you, you're beet red!"

My head's about to explode as I will her to stop talking.

"Why are you beet red?" Ari asks, confused.

"I'm not, Ari. No worries. Hey, you wanna watch Netflix?"

He nods. "Yes, *SpongeBob*."

Good. *SpongeBob* is the answer to all the world's problems. We all get up to go the family room.

"Totally wants you," Abby says.

"Stop," I argue. "You're wrong."

"Mm-hmm. Denial," she says as she flops onto the sofa and puts her feet on the coffee table, "ain't just a river in Egypt."

I ignore this comment, and turn on *SpongeBob*. Besides, it's not denial. I fully admit that I am attracted to Eli Costas. I just need to get over it. Now.

He doesn't get home with his parents until long after midnight. I run to the bathroom window when I hear MJ rattle up the driveway. Mr. Costas hops out of Eli's truck and then makes his way to their car behind it. Both Mr. and Mrs. Costas help him out, handing him a pair of crutches.

My heart sinks. And hurts, too. I know Eli so well. I know how much this season means. Meant. I also know he doesn't think he has any other prospects in life except for lacrosse, and that kills me. He's got so much going for him. I wish he believed it, too.

I watch them go to the back of the house. My mom opens the door for them. She went over when she got back from class so that Ari could get to bed. I consider going downstairs when she gets home and getting the details from her, but I know whatever happened, it's bad.

I want to text him, let him know I'm here. Then I think of what Abby said tonight, how she thinks he likes me—how she thinks I like him. Does he? Does he like me? I mean *like me*, like me? It's not possible. *I'm* the one who, regardless of my hypothesis, can't stop thinking about him.

I can't text him. Can I?

I don't need to answer that, because he texts me first.

Torn ACL and meniscus. Season over. :(

I'm so sorry. Lots of pain?

Nah. MRI Monday. Can you get a ride?

Of course, don't worry about me.

Sorry, habit.

Habit. My habit is fantasizing about him shirtless, his habit is making sure I'm okay.

I'm a bad person.

I go back to bed, reminding myself how no matter how Eli makes me feel, I can't give up on science. I can't. It's the only thing you can count on. The kiss—I've got to find the guy who does it right. When I do, Eli will still be in my life, but he will just be my friend. For real, just friends.

That will mean I can worry about him and care about him. Even love him. I just can't be his. He can't be mine—and that has to be okay.

Chapter Fourteen

The bed I'm lying on gets swallowed up in the MRI machine. Some people freak out about being shoved in a tube for however long it takes to get a picture of a body part, but I don't care. I'm used to it.

It's Monday, tomorrow is the game, and if it wasn't obvious, I won't be playing. I can't think too much about that. For the last couple of days, I've been thinking about my future. It's pretty dismal. Coach came to see me and told me not to worry, he'd talk to the coach from State. I'm not holding my breath. I've been here before and it sucks. Surgery. Rehab. Maybe if I do the fast-track rehab like I did last time, work my ass off, then I could be cleared to play in time for the college season.

I exhale, hard.

"Please don't move, Eli," the technician speaks over an intercom.

"Sorry," I mumble without moving my lips.

The one bright spot—Nora. On Saturday, she made her mom drive her all the way out to the Tick Tock and she brought me one of those pies, the black bottom one. It was probably the nicest thing anyone has ever done for me. She didn't just deliver it, either—she came to my room with the whole pie and two forks. Her hair was down, she was wearing some type of dress with strappy things holding it up. It was flowered and floaty, and I imagined things. Who could blame me? I haven't seen her in a dress in a while. I was also on some major painkillers, but I remember exactly what I said:

"Wow. You should wear dresses more often."

She instantly narrowed her eyes, again. "Why? What's wrong with it?"

I shook my head. "Why can't you just take a compliment?"

She shrugged, sat down on the edge of my bed, and handed me a fork. We observed a moment of silence as we ogled the pie.

She let me taste first.

"I *can* take a compliment, by the way," she said. "Just not from you, for some reason."

I dug my fork in. "That's weird," I said. "Well, you look hot today. Deal with it."

She turned bright pink. "Okay, that's enough."

"What, can't I say you look hot?"

"*No,*" she said, but for a long time she was quiet, like she was absorbing the words, and maybe they made her feel good.

They had the same effect on me, but in a way that made me want to pull her across the bed and kiss her like that eighth grade version of me never could've handled. Of course, I didn't do that. I put all that energy into eating that pie.

Anyway, Nora's visit at least took my mind off my other problem—the knee. Which is why I'm here. The machine is loud and it doesn't bother me. In fact, I kind of like it. It's nice to be totally isolated, to have some time to think about whatever I want.

Right now, I want to think about her.

The only other choice is the season, and how I'm probably gonna have to be an accountant or some shit like that because my plans for playing lacrosse are shot to hell.

I can't be an accountant. I totally suck at math.

The machine makes a sound like an airplane trying to take off, so I let myself go, like I'm going airborne, and she's there. In that dress. Nora who doesn't want me, and likes me, but doesn't like me. Can't like me. Because of science.

I hoped I was making headway with her. Now I think it might be impossible to change her mind. This plan of mine might be a lost cause.

God, she's beautiful.

I told her she was hot, which doesn't even begin to cover it. I don't even think I can put it into words. Most people, like her mom, my parents, and even Gigi, treat us like we're brother and sister. It's a good thing they're not in my brain right now or they'd think I'm the biggest pervert on the planet.

She is so beautiful. Maybe not in a way that slays everyone, not like a supermodel, but I've always liked her face. It's interesting. I know I'm eighteen, a guy, and I'm supposedly only into tits and ass—which I know she also has, special thanks to that bikini. I liked all of that, too, except with her, there's more.

She's got that strange brain, and she makes me laugh more than anyone else literally on the planet. She can talk about anything, and it's not like I'm a big talker, but I can talk to her, and she listens. I love the way she wants to help every person, every animal, the whole damn planet. How she knows my brother so well that it never gets awkward or weird. She knows his limits, and she loves him. She cares so much about her grandma, and her mom, and even her dad, who has to be the biggest deadbeat on earth. I love the way she almost gets killed running into traffic to save a cat.

Also, she's brilliant. So much smarter than me. Always trying to figure out how things work, or why they don't. Brilliant.

All I'm saying is, it's the whole package with her.

The machine makes a *chunk-whirr* sound as the magnetos—or whatever the hell they are—burrow into my knee, and I remember things.

I close my eyes tight and remember a day when we were twelve. Gigi took us to Silver Springs, this big state park nearby. She did it to get me out of the house, I'm sure of this. My parents were fighting a lot—Ari had just been diagnosed and I think they blamed themselves that he wasn't "normal" or whatever.

Life was a total shit show.

Nora knew what was going on—we didn't keep things from each other back then (like now, apparently).

That morning, when we packed up Gigi's old station wagon, Nora leaned toward me, smiling. "Okay, Eli," she said. "Today, we are leaving this world and going through a portal to paradise."

"You're weird," was my reply. That was my standard reply back then. Of course, she was right. She is always right.

There were mad colors at the park, loud greens that you could never find in your box of Crayolas, and giant pink flowers on steroids, their middles orangey yellow. We got ice cream, bright-white vanilla with giant red strawberries on top, and there was this glass-bottom boat ride. It took you out on a river, to the natural springs that the place is named for. That water was such a bright, clear blue, and so deep. I wondered what would happen if our boat got sucked into one of those springs, like a real portal that would drop us in a new place where life was easy, where parents didn't fight, where brothers weren't picked on by idiots because they were different.

I was sitting next to her on that boat, and she touched me, laid her hand on my back as I gazed through the glass floor. It was like she was sharing my sadness, like she was trying to take it from me. She understood. I turned to her, and she didn't move her hand. I remember thinking, if this boat got sucked into another world, it would be just fine, because Nora Reid would be there with me.

It was like when we were in the water the other day at the beach. Just the two of us. For a few minutes, it was like we got sucked into another world again, a place where she could actually love me.

Did she know how close I was to kissing her? For a nanosecond I thought, *yeah, she wants this as bad as you do. DO IT.*

But I couldn't. This isn't about what I want, this is about teaching her that her hypothesis is bull. That garage kiss we had has to be the *only* kiss between us until she falls for me totally and completely. Once that happens, she'll believe what I've been trying to tell her—the lightning bolt, the earthquake, whatever the hell it is she's looking for, can happen, even after a shit first kiss. She'll see she's been wrong. Then she can get on with her life, mission accomplished.

So I'm not going to kiss her anytime soon, if ever, but for the time I have left in this tube, I will let myself imagine what could happen if I did. I go back to my room on Saturday, and remember how I wanted to throw that pie on the floor, take her in my arms, and say, "I'm going to kiss you, and this kiss is gonna move the earth." Then I say, "If that's okay with you." Because you gotta ask.

That's when she smiles and dips her chin, and her hair falls forward and I take her in my arms and I kiss her and it's good. Real good. I don't stop there. I lift the dress up and over her head and kiss everywhere. She doesn't stop me.

Hypothesis. Disproved.

Heh. It's nice, and dammit, I'm not giving up on this plan of mine. I might fail, but if I succeed, it'll be worth it. Success is the only outcome in which I get to kiss Nora Reid again.

The machine falls silent. I come back to the real world and remember that I'm only wearing this cloth-gown thing and I'm not in this tube far enough and I don't want every tech in the joint to know that I'm having MRI sex fantasies. So I quickly start thinking of lacrosse plays, running through them in my head, and shit, is lacrosse really over for me? Please don't let it be over.

By the time they pull me out of the tube, no one can tell that I've been dreaming about Nora.

All they can tell me is that yeah, I need surgery, and yes, my season is totally over. Then everything goes to hell when Mom gives me back my phone and there's a text from Koviak.

Tex been talking about asking out N. U want me to do something?

Damn it, why is my whole life going down the shitter? I need to fix this, fast.

Chapter Fifteen

Nora

It's been a long week. Eli was out of school through Wednesday getting the MRI and driving to Gainesville to see the orthopedist. I tell him I'll help him with his missed work, if he wants. I don't expect him to take me up on that. Homework isn't a priority with him.

Another thing that happened this week—Caleb and I have been texting—a lot. He's interested, and so cute. I know I need to follow through. Now I get a text from Eli.

Party at o'dells 2morrow night? Time for another lesson? Night driving practice v important

I'm surprised, and also a little nervous about being alone with him. I've been thinking about him a lot, mostly because of the knee, and because he told me I was hot.

When he said that, I *felt* it. I felt *hot*. All over. But then there was pie, and the moment was over, mostly. Since then, he's made it into more than the usual amount of my dreams, which have also definitely been *hot.*

All the more reason to say no to this party. Plus, O'Dell's is a big old hunting lodge out in the middle of nowhere. It's famous for out-of-control parties and I'm not fond of anything that's out of control *or* of driving in the dark.

What about knee?

Crutches work. What say you?

I say NO! Say it, Nora, SAY IT!

Do I have to?

Need someone to hold my crutches while I play beer pong.

I don't respond.

It will be fun. And driving test coming up.

Again, I'm silent, trying to figure out how to stand my ground.

Come on. Senior yr.... YOLO, babe. Amirite?

Okay. Get some sleep weirdo. don't call me babe.

God, I'm the weakest of weaklings.

The next night, Eli hobbles out of the house on the arm of his mom who helps him limp toward our garage. My mom comes out, too, almost giddy. She's so happy I'm being more social that it's freaking me out. I still haven't told her I've been driving, just like Emory feels like it needs to stay a necessary secret, for now. Not that I'm afraid of her reaction. I just don't want to rock the boat when it doesn't need to be rocked. I feel the same about telling Eli. Keep the waters calm. Put on the lifejackets only if needed.

"You sure you're okay to drive, honey?" my mom asks Eli.

He beams at my mother, liberally spreading that Eli charm like fertilizer. "Yes, ma'am. Right leg works great. Haven't taken any painkillers today, so I'm safe to operate large machinery."

Mom laughs, completely snowed by him.

Mrs. Costas looks worried. "All right, you two, have fun, and be careful, Eli. I really think this is too soon."

"Mom, I'll be fine, trust me." She isn't as easily charmed, though. I wonder if the Costas charm comes from his father and between the two of them, his mom has been on the receiving end of it long enough to be immune.

I wonder if I'll ever be immune to Eli.

She frowns. "Absolutely no drinking, Eli." She winks at me. "You've got precious cargo with you." They still treat us like we're eight.

He grumbles. She bends in through the car door and gives him a kiss on the cheek. "God, Ma, I get it. I'll be careful." His jaw tenses as he starts the engine and backs down the driveway.

He adjusts the rearview mirror. "I guess it doesn't qualify as 'precious cargo' when it's just me?" he says.

"She's got another son," I say. "You're easily replaced."

"Sadly true. They like him much better anyway."

I snicker. "Can you blame them?" As he backs my car out, and our mothers wave good-bye to us—which we don't acknowledge—I smooth my hair and try to calm my nerves. I'm nervous about everything—about driving, this party, being with Eli. "How's the knee today?" I ask.

He hesitates. "It's fine. Just sucks, you know."

I do know—I hate that this has happened to him. "Yeah."

"Hey," he says. "You look nice tonight."

I keep my eyes forward out the windshield. What's with him and making comments on my clothes? I pick at the shirt I'm wearing. "Oh." It's just a lightweight button-down top with jeans shorts, because it's still so hot out. I almost ask what he really means by that, but then I realize that this is a compliment, and I should be able to take a compliment from a friend.

I sit up straighter. "Thank you."

Eli pulls into the Mermaid and parks. I don't want to drive, but that's the main reason I've agreed to go to the party in the first place. Plus Caleb's supposed to be there.

That doesn't stop a lump of fear from forming in my throat when I get behind the wheel. My hands start to sweat and my stomach churns. *Clear your mind, Nora. It's fifteen miles to O'Dell's. That's three sets of five miles. You can drive five miles with your eyes closed.* A trickle of fear crawls up my spine. Driving with my eyes closed would be a bad idea.

"All right," Eli says, way too excited. "Let's go!"

I put the car in reverse…and that's about it.

He leans in, close to my ear. "Go!" he whispers firmly.

I swallow hard, my mouth is doing that tingly pre-puke thing. I hit that woman's leg in the dark. Maybe I should just not drive at night?

Fifteen miles. Fifteen miles. Fifteen miles. "Okay," I say, "backing up now." I pull out of the spot slowly, too slowly judging from the depth of Eli's groan.

"Stop with the noises and talk to me," I say, and he does. In fact, he starts and doesn't stop. He talks about the homework he's missed and the movie he took Ari to this week, and the fact that the CSU coach didn't even show up at the game Tuesday like he was supposed to. The Highlanders lost, he tells me, but not by much. He was there, on his crutches, cheering them on, although he hated being on the sidelines, not in the action.

He keeps chatting and before I know it, we're three sets of five miles out in the middle of the country, parked along a dirt road with about a hundred other cars.

"I did it," I say, mostly to myself.

"You're definitely getting better. You feel more confident?"

My pulse is at a normal range. I'm not about to hyperventilate. I take the keys out of the ignition. "Yeah. I think so."

"You need more practice, but don't worry, you'll get there." He opens his door. "Let's do this."

Now I feel my pulse start to race. I open my door. "Let's get it over with."

We have to walk a while to reach the house, and the crutches slow us down. On the way in, we merge with a few small groups of kids who are also arriving, most of whom I know. They all greet Eli in a variety of ways—a pat on the back, a shaken hand, a flirty look, a hair flip. They're polite to me, but he gets the full celebrity treatment. Everyone asks about his knee and if he's going to play this season.

I need to lighten his mood, which I can tell is turning sour. "You wanted to come for the sympathy flirting, didn't you?"

"Yeah. It's awesome." His voice is pure sarcasm. I hold the door open and he and I move into the cavernous front room. It's decorated in hunting-lodge chic with stuffed animal heads all over the walls, and it reeks of beer. A basic nightmare.

"Can I just remind you," I say to him, "you said we didn't have to stay long."

"We don't. Just promise you'll try to have fun, okay?"

I check out the crowd. So many people. "Okay, just don't

disappear on me."

"I won't. But you'll try, right?"

He wobbles on his crutches and I reach out to grab his arm. When I do I feel a spark. We both jump and I squeak. "Static," I explain.

He gives me the smile. Adds in the dimple. "Electricity."

"Dude!" I hear Koviak before I see him, plowing toward us through the crowd. "What's up?" He gives Eli a man-hug and then turns my way. "Nora, haven't seen you at one of these in a while. Welcome."

He's smiling, and I almost actually believe that he's being sincere.

"Oh my God, Nora!" Someone yells. I turn to find the source and see Abby waving at me from the kitchen. She waves me over. "Come here!"

I go to "here," which is where the keg is set up. Abby's standing in a puddle of beer, filling a red plastic cup.

Her eyes trail behind me and I know she's looking at Eli. "What are you doing here?" Again, she looks over my shoulder and grins. "You came in together. It finally happened? Did you two finally hook up? Mmm-hmm. I knew it!"

I can't believe her. She never stops. "No! Abby, we're not here together, okay? We drove, together, that's it. Why are you here? Aren't you still grounded?"

She drops the tap and screws up her mouth. She won't look at me.

"What's wrong?" I ask.

She scratches the side of her face, holds out the beer. "Here, pumped it just for you."

I watch her, wondering why she's acting so weird. "What's going on, Abby?"

"So...I might have told my mom that I was at your house."

"You did? Why?"

She's swaying a little, like she's already had too much to

drink. "Because when it comes to you, Mom totally doesn't question anything." She leans into me. "I don't know what it is, but don't ever lose it. At least not for the next five months." She tugs the bottom of my shirt and winks. "I might need to use it again."

Anger bubbles up inside of me. Abby and I had so much in common, once, but I wouldn't do that to anyone, especially a friend. Plus, she could have invited me to this party. Instead, she used me as a cover story. Maybe that's all I am to her.

She steps back. "Oh God, are you mad? No! NO! Stop it, Nor, I love you, you know that. You and me, we're like sisters from a different mister." She moves closer, tilts her head toward mine. "Like, you and I are smarter than the rest of the school put together. Right? I would go insane without your brain." Her rhyme cracks her up, and she takes the beer out of my hand when she sees I'm not drinking it. "You just don't like to party, which is fine, no judgment. But I wanted to come, so I needed to give Mom a name."

"*My* name?"

She screws up her mouth. "Yes. I really didn't think you'd mind, Nora. It's not like it's hurting you."

It does hurt, though. "I gotta go, Abby." I take the beer out of her hand and I walk away.

"Don't be like that, Nor!" she calls after me. I ignore her and keep walking, feeling terrible, like I don't have one real friend at this party, except for Eli and he's disappeared. That didn't take long. I want to leave already, but we've been here for less than ten minutes and most of that was walking from my car to the front door.

I wind my way through some hallways jammed with people, and look for a place to hide.

I open one door—a powder room. Another door—a packed closet. The last door opens into a laundry room— no bodies in here. I step inside and close the door behind me. A minute later, I hear a familiar voice on the other side. Veronica? She was actually nice to me at the beach.

"He's so hot," she says.

"So hot," another voice echoes. "Do you think they're together?"

"No. They're neighbors." That's Veronica talking. "He has to drive her around because she's banned from getting a license. He couldn't wait to get away from her when they got here. Did you see that?" She laughs like a witch.

"Why'd she even come?" the other voice says. "She hates us."

"And God, what's with her hair anyway? Does she actually think it looks good?"

"I'm sure she does."

Now they both laugh.

Now. *Now* I'm ready to leave, except there's no way I'm walking out there, right through them. There's a door on the other side of the washing machine, hopefully an exit. I open it—the garage. Its dark in here, but I don't care. I light up the space with my phone. There's an old car with no tires that, like the rest of this place, looks like it hasn't been touched in decades. It's unlocked, so I sit sideways on the driver's seat and text Eli.

I'm ready to go I type, but don't hit send right away, knowing he'll give me a hard time about leaving so soon.

I look at my phone, at pictures of this party that are spreading online like wildfire. There's Veronica Peele's Snapchat story, featuring her face in a series of selfies with just about every boy in school. Veronica who was once my friend, back in middle school. Why does she think I hate her? *She* hates *me*. And was that true, what she said? Could Eli not wait to get away from me? I have no idea where he is right now, or what he's doing. He could be drinking. He could be having sex.

I hit send on the text. A few seconds later, I get a response.

Where are you?

Garage

I never should have come tonight. I brush the concrete floor with my shoe—I know it's my theory that's gotten me to this place, hiding in the dark in the middle of a huge party with people who used to be my friends. Proving a hypothesis doesn't always make you popular, but I'm committed to it, no matter what the cost.

Chapter Sixteen

Eli

I flip a switch that turns on a bare lightbulb hanging from the ceiling. "This is what you call trying?"

She's sitting sideways in the front seat of an old red hatchback, her feet hanging out. "I *did* try," she says. "It didn't work out."

I rock back and forth on my crutches. "Wow. You gave it a whole five minutes."

"More like fifteen—but yes."

I maneuver the perimeter of the garage, which isn't easy. There's a workbench piled high with old tools. Next to it, an ancient green refrigerator. "Hey look," I say, "just like eighth grade. Heh. Wonder if there's a Coke in here." I pull it open. Empty. "Don't worry," I close it again. "We won't relive the past. Fridge smells like death."

"Great. You're going to make fun of me, too? And thanks for not disappearing." She pulls her legs into the car and slams the door.

Dammit. She's right. I told her I'd stay close, then she walked away, and then I saw Tex and was trying to keep him busy, away from her.

She's got her head down in there. I hope she's not crying. I hate when she cries. I hoist my lame self around to the passenger side. It's some old Chevy, a model I don't recognize, rusty and falling apart. I open the door, hop inside, and fling my crutches to the floor.

"I wasn't making fun of you."

"I don't want to talk," she says.

"Okay, let's not talk." I close my door.

She sighs and then makes a growling sound. "I hate my life." She digs in her purse and pulls out a hair thingy, starts to gather up her hair. Without thinking, I snatch it out of her hand.

"What are you doing?" she says. "Give me that."

I pass it to my right hand, out of her reach. "No."

She scowls. "It's mine. Give it to me."

I shake my head. "No. I like your hair down."

She turns forward and grips the steering wheel. "Why do you keep bringing up my hair? It's weird."

I don't get it, either. "Yeah, it is. I have no explanation."

She turns to me again. Honestly, I'm a little scared right now, but I push forward. Now's not the time to be a chickenshit.

I lean my body toward her, just an inch or two. "Why do you hate your life?" I ask.

Her lips press together and she shrugs. "I don't know? Because it sucks. I have no friends. Mom's a mess. Gigi. And…college." She freezes, and I think, now, now she'll tell me.

I stare at her. "What about college?"

Her body shifts forward again. "Nothing."

That's it. Enough is enough.

"It's not nothing, Nora. You got accepted to Emory, and it's one of the best programs in the country."

Her eyes almost bug out of her head. *Gotcha.*

"What?"

"Yeah, I know. I saw that printout that Chaffee gave you. The scholarship thing." I slap a rhythm on the dashboard. "Ha! I've known all along."

She's silent for a few second, lowers her head. "I haven't gotten any scholarships." Her voice is soft. "That's why I didn't tell you."

It's close in here, to the point of distraction, but I have to focus. "Whatever. I just figured maybe we've gotten to the point where we're not gonna tell each other everything anymore." My voice sounds sad and I'm working that Costas charm, keeping my eye on the goal. "It's okay. Doesn't mean we're not friends."

"No." She gulps. "That's not it." There's a beer in the cup holder between us and she taps its rim with her finger. "It wasn't our plan and I didn't want to say anything. I don't even think it's going to happen." Her gaze comes back to me. "I should have told you. Please don't be mad."

I nod, recognizing that I need to proceed with caution. "No, I get it. I mean, I was pissed at first. Then this week, when I was just lying around, I went to my favorite internet source, Wikipedia, and learned all about the Emory Eagles. That place is a big deal. Also, hard to get into. Like twenty-five percent acceptance rate. You know what that means?"

She exhales, maybe she's relieved? I can't tell, but her eyes are definitely doing that sparkling thing that they do.

"Yeah, I do."

"That means, that for seventy-five percent of the kids who apply, Emory is all like, nah, you're stupid. Get lost."

The corners of her mouth are turned up slightly. "I might not get any scholarships. It's really expensive, and if I don't get enough money, I can't go. I haven't told Mom, either. It's not worth worrying her yet."

"Do you *want* to go?" My stomach turns over. I don't know if I want to hear the answer.

She pushes back her hair. "I don't know. I'm worried about leaving Mom and Gigi. Ari. Marie. Home…"

It's a long list and I'm not on it.

"Don't worry about me, I'll be fine." I tilt my head, hit her with the smile, and throw in the dimples as a bonus.

She does that thing, lowering her eyelids, slowly, like they've got weights attached. It's sexy.

"No," she says, her voice going an octave deeper like it does when she's serious. "And you. I'd miss you."

I suck in those words like they're oxygen and I'm about to drown. "You would? Really?"

Her eyes drop again. "Yes. Really. Of course."

"Huh." I turn away, peer out into the dim garage.

"What?"

I brace myself. It's time to make my move. I face her again. "Maybe it's being in a garage with you again. It's messing with my head."

Anger flashes in her eyes. "Why do you have to bring that up?"

Shit. This whole plan of mine, it feels like a dance. I'm trying to get the steps right, but I think I'm always about to fall on my ass.

"I don't know," I say. "Not like it's my favorite memory."

She laughs low. "No. Mine either. I had such a huge crush on you then."

I can't believe she just said that.

"You did not."

Her eyebrows pull together. "Why do you think I kissed you?"

"Because I was your first test case?"

The corners of her mouth curve up slightly. "No. It wasn't an experiment, not yet, not back then. I didn't think there'd be anyone else. I thought you were the only one."

She lifts the plastic cup from the drink holder, takes a sip, makes a face and shudders. "Beer is disgusting," she says.

I don't want to talk about beer. "What if I had been?"

"Been what?"

"The One. What if you'd felt it, back then? The lightning strike. We were only thirteen," I say, skeptical. "What would have happened to us?"

She lifts her hands. "I guess we would have been like Romeo and Juliet."

"Double murder suicide?"

She pushes my shoulder. "No! I mean"—she pauses— "young lovers."

"Oh." I twist in my seat, trying not to get excited thinking of us as lovers, young or otherwise. "You're seriously missing the point of that story, you know."

"Which is?"

I pause, put a finger to my mouth, thinking. "What was Willie's point?"

"Willie?"

I give her the smile again—I'm on to something here. "Willie Shakespeare, my literary bro?"

She purses her lips, not buying my bullshit.

"You doubt me? You might be surprised to know I've got an eighty-four average in English. So, pretty much top of the class. So for Will, it was all about the tragedy. Star-crossed lovers. No happy endings."

"Right," she agrees. "So depressing." She glances out her side window. Her hair moves with her. I want to touch it.

Keep going, Costas. "It's only depressing if you kill yourself over it. Love doesn't always work out. Shit happens. That's life."

She doesn't respond, but turns back to me again. God, those eyes. I can't control myself. I reach out and touch her hair, hold a lock of it between my fingers. She doesn't move, doesn't take her eyes off of me, doesn't ask what I'm doing, doesn't tell me to stop. I have her attention.

"That's what makes it so good," I say. "When you find it, and it's right—and I think you can know it's right. Even without an earthquake, I think you can know, not that it's going to last forever, but that it's at least worth a try."

Her eyes, they're sucking me in, they're the bottom of the glass boat, a window to another world. They close slowly again, and open, like a butterfly's wings.

Nora is worth a try. "What about science?" she whispers. She's moved closer, I think, and it's getting hot in this car. I swallow hard. Got to keep my head.

"I told you." I've still got her hair, holding it tight. She still doesn't stop me. "It's not science. It's chaos."

"Chaos?"

She closes the space between us. Nora and me, we're sharing the same air, lips about to touch, again. My body is sending me signals. I don't want to stop. Every fantasy I've had about kissing her, touching her, flashes through my head, and all I can think about is how maybe, just maybe, every one of them might have a chance to come true if I just lean in and take what I want. What I'm pretty sure she wants, too.

Hey, dumbass, you can't kiss her.

Moment. Destroyed.

I pull back, which is the hardest thing I've ever done. "Uhh..."

She comes to, jerks away from me, smoothes her hair, and flings open the door. "Sorry," she says. "I'm. I'm a little..." She scans the interior of the car wildly. "I had a beer."

I see her beer. It's full.

My body slumps, utterly exhausted. This plan of mine is

taking its toll on me. "Okay," I say. "Nor, look." I need to be careful, but I have no idea what I'm saying anymore. "I had a crush on you, too, back then, back in Madison's garage. Man, it was a bad crush."

"You did?" Her voice is small. I'm making her uncomfortable.

"Yeah. I was too much of a chickenshit to do anything about it, then you kissed me, and it sucked, and you shut me down. I never had a chance."

She won't look at me all of a sudden. Is she even listening? I move my hand, touch her cheek, lift her face until I have her attention again. "Nora?"

There she is.

"I'm not a chickenshit anymore."

She looks confused, not sure what's happening. If I'm honest, I feel the same way, but I can't let that stop me.

"Nora, if I ever get a chance to kiss you again, it won't be because you're having a moment of weakness, or because you're scared maybe your theory is wrong."

She bites her lip, and the movement is like the fucking Death Star tractor beam. But I'm not done.

"If we kiss again, *when* we kiss again, it'll be because you're done experimenting, and you know who you've been looking for."

Her eyes drill into mine, it's like I can see her brain processing my words. Did I really just say all that? I lower my hand, and she turns forward, with that same terrified look she gets when she has to drive. What have I done?

She steps out of the car. "I'm sorry, Eli. I'm so sorry."

That's it. I'm sunk. I watch her walk around the car to my side, apologizing the whole way around. "It's okay," I say, though it's not clear what she's sorry about. She helps me with my crutches, I can see she's shaken. So am I.

As we make our way out, the irony of this happening

again, in another garage, with her, is not lost on me.

I step into the laundry room and my eyes adjust to the bright light. In front of me are Eddie Ponti, going through a cabinet above the dryer, and—*shit*—Tex.

"Costas!" Eddie yells. "You seen cups? We need cups!"

I'm about to answer when Nora appears next to me. Eddie's face lights up like he's just seen goddamn Santa Claus. "Heeeey, Nora," he says, never taking his eyes off me. I know what this looks like.

Tex looks at Nora and doesn't stop. I don't like it.

"You two have fun out there?" Ponti laughs, the asshole.

Tex catches up to what's going on and his face gets all serious like his cow ran away.

"Shut it," I say to Ed.

"Yes, we had fun," Nora says in her matter-of-fact, don't-fuck-with-me tone. She glares at Eddie. "We're friends, Ed. We had fun, talking. Just because a male and a female are alone together doesn't mean they must be having sex. If any girl would ever agree to be alone with you, you would know that."

The corner of Tex's mouth curls up on one side. Asshole cowboy face.

"Fine." Eddie wisely doesn't try to defend himself. He clears a space for us to walk through. "Sorry."

"Hey, Nora," Tex drawls. "Can I get you a beer?"

"You know what?" I don't give her a chance to answer. "My knee's killing me." I'm not proud of lying to a teammate, but I can't deal with this shithead for another minute. "We gotta go."

"I can take you home," he says to Nora.

I'm going to kick his ass.

"No thanks, Caleb," Nora says. "I drove us."

"Okay," he says. "You wanna do something this week?"

"Maybe," she says, biting her bottom lip.

Tex doesn't give up, the douchebag. "There's a JV game Thursday. I was gonna go. We could go together, maybe get some dinner after?"

No. I'm willing her to say it. *Please. Say no.*

Is it me, or does she look like a deer in headlights? "All right, just text me," she says. She sounds like she can't get away from him fast enough. Why didn't she say no?

She follows me out to the main room, where about twenty more people ask about my knee. I'm about to go full-on Incredible Hulk by the time we finally get outside.

Nora helps me down the porch stairs and I can't move. I'm frozen with panic. Did I just destroy any chance I had with her, coming on to her like that? What is with me? It was like I had diarrhea of the mouth in that car. I couldn't stop. I should've stopped.

Now she's gonna go on a date with that Lone Star–state dillweed. She stops walking when she notices I'm not moving. "What is it? Eli?" She rushes back to my side, her voice panicky. "You should have told me your knee was hurting. I'll go get the car. Don't move."

I nod, once, and watch her run down the gravel road. My knee doesn't hurt, not at all, but I can't move. It's like my body has gone into shock, trying to absorb what my heart just realized.

That girl...the one running away who wants nothing to do with me? I love her.

I love Nora Reid.

Chapter Seventeen

I can barely fill my lungs as I run to the car. What just happened?

The scene plays over and over in my head.

I almost *kissed* him. I *wanted* to kiss him. What is wrong with me?

On the way home along the pitch black of the country road, I try to focus on not creating any road kill. Focus on getting Eli back because his knee hurts. All I can think about is what he said back there.

He's quiet now. Why isn't he talking? Why did he say we would kiss again? He wants to kiss me? Didn't he say that?

The silence is freaking me out. I'm trying to think of something, anything normal, to say, but my mind is like a black hole. I want to talk about what just happened in the garage, and also, I never want to speak of it again.

"Center yourself in the lane. You're drifting."

Finally, there's talking.

"Okay," I say, though I felt like I was pretty much in the center. I nudge the car a little to the right.

"When are you taking the test?" he asks.

"Next Friday. I already made the appointment. Just need to tell my mom first."

"And when are you gonna tell her about Emory?"

My jaw tightens and I grip the steering wheel harder. "I want to wait until I hear about scholarships, and then I'll tell her."

"Good, you should. I bet it'll make her happy."

I wish I had his confidence. "I don't know. This fall was so bad, moving Gigi." I concentrate on making a tight corner, which I navigate perfectly. "She already has too much to handle. I just want to know for sure, so she doesn't have another thing to worry about."

He's silent for an endless minute. "Why did you apply?"

This conversation is quickly morphing into a confession. Maybe we would have been better off not talking. "Mr. Chaffee told me about their program, and I researched it. Then I got sort of excited. I was doubtful they'd want me. He thought I had a good chance, though. He wrote me a recommendation, and they accepted me."

"Cool. The only thing he ever wrote me was a tardy slip."

He's trying to be funny, but I don't laugh. "I did it on a whim, really. To see if I could get in."

"You could have gotten in anywhere. Everywhere."

I focus on the road. I don't want to talk about Emory. "Maybe. I'm not sure if it's right to leave Mom now, though, even if I do get a decent scholarship."

He moves his leg, trying to get comfortable, maybe. "You're always doing that. Looking out for her. She's stronger than you think, though. I bet she'll be fine."

"Maybe," I say, not sure that's true.

"So…" He pauses. "Maybe we can fit a few more lessons

in before the surgery?"

My grip tightens on the steering wheel. "More?"

I know. I know. I should not agree to spend more time with him, even for driving lessons. That's a no-brainer. I should wait for Tex's call and go out with *him*. I could practically feel the sparks coming off him in that laundry room.

Except that right now, all I can think about are the sparks between me and Eli in that garage, and how close I came to kissing him. I need to say no.

My mind goes blank. "Yeah, okay," I say. Apparently, my brain is set to self-destruct. "Just a few more."

"Whatever you want," he says.

That's the problem, right there in a nutshell. What I *want* is him.

By the time we get back to the Mermaid, we're in silent mode again, lost in our own thoughts. At least I am.

"Ready to switch?" I ask.

"Yeah."

I pull the crutches out of the backseat and help him out, realizing that I just drove the whole way home without even thinking about the driving part of it.

The Mermaid is still open, and pie sounds so good right now. I glance at Eli sideways. It's not a good idea, not tonight. Sure, we'd eventually find things to talk about—lacrosse, Emory, scholarships, family, and friends. It's the things that won't be said that I can't stop thinking about, things that are threatening to derail me, my hypothesis, possibly my whole life.

As he gets back in and I take his crutches, he looks back toward the restaurant, too, probably coming to the same conclusion. I close my door and without a word he pulls away, out of the parking lot, driving too fast.

I'm about to tell him to slow down when I see blue-and-red lights in my side mirror. Hear the *whoop, whoop* of a police car.

"Perfect." He pulls over.

I'm not sure what he expected, driving like a maniac.

"Shit." He puts the car in park and glances at the side mirror. "It's my dad. Of course."

Eli lowers the window and Mr. Costas leans inside. "Nora." He speaks like Eli isn't even there. "I'm sorry my son is driving your car, or any car, like he's on the NASCAR circuit."

"Hi, Mr. Costas."

He finally acknowledges Eli. "You been drinking?"

Eli stays quiet, his eyes forward. "No."

"Do I need to check?"

He clenches his teeth. "No. You don't."

"All right," Mr. Costas says. "I'm going to give you a ticket."

Eli's mouth drops open. "What?"

His father holds out a hand. "License and registration."

"You've got to be kidding me," Eli snaps.

Mr. Costas is not kidding, not at all. It's kind of obvious.

"What? You really think I'm going to give you a pass, just because you're my kid? You can pay the fine, then go to defensive driving school. Won't hurt you. Might prevent this from happening again."

When his father goes back to the cruiser, I guess to write the ticket, Eli smacks the steering wheel. "Every cop in this town would have let me go with a warning. Not him." He turns his body toward me. "See, that's why you should tell your mom about Emory."

"Why?"

He scowls. "Because I have nothing like that to tell him.

Not only am I not smart enough to get into real college, now I can't even play the game that he's spent all this money on since I was four. Now it's like he expects me to screw up. I can't do anything to make him proud. Your mom might freak about you leaving, but you gotta tell her. Parents live for that shit." He adjusts the rearview mirror. "So I hear, anyway."

Mr. Costas brings back a ticket, passes it through the window, and Eli drives away, without a word.

A few minutes later, we pull up the driveway and into the garage. Our kitchen light is on. His house is all lit up, everyone is still awake. For all that happened at that party, we weren't gone for very long. Eli turns off the engine. We're in a dark garage again, which feels dangerous.

His head hangs low and his hands still grip the wheel. "Sorry about tonight."

What's he sorry about? That we almost kissed? Or that he stopped it? I guess I spend too long analyzing, because he opens his door.

"All right," he says. "Good night."

"Wait." I lay my hand on his arm. His skin is warm, and it seems to transfer through to my body. I can't look directly at him, but I feel him watching me, setting my whole body on fire. I am trying so hard to act cool. I'm afraid that he'll know that something happened inside of me tonight, something shifted, even if it was temporary. "Don't be sorry."

I lift my eyes and meet his.

His forehead furrows, and I feel the sparks starting up again. I know he's wondering what the hell that meant. So am I. I've believed in my hypothesis for so long, been so rigid about it, and then I almost kissed him tonight. For real, if he hadn't stopped it, something would have happened. I can't explain any of this to him so I throw open my door and get out.

I gather his crutches from the backseat and hand them

over, staying near in case he needs me.

My face feels so hot; I'm glad it's dark in here. When he's out, I'm tempted to give him a hug, just a friendly hug, thanking him for the evening. I'm just not sure I can be that close to him right now. I'm not sure it's safe. Instead I lift a hand and pat the side of his arm.

"Okay," he whispers, one corner of his mouth turns up.

"Okay."

"We'll talk about the next lesson tomorrow?" His voice sounds hopeful, or maybe that's wishful thinking.

Say NO, Nora. It's not too late. This is happening because of you—what kind of intelligent woman tries to get over someone by spending more time with him?

I ignore the flurry of warnings in my head. "Okay, yes." I say, because I am an idiot.

We walk out of the garage, together, safe now. Nothing is going to happen out in the open.

His mom steps out their back door, arms crossed. "A ticket? Really?"

"Great," he mumbles as he hobbles toward his house. "Night, Nora."

"Good night." I head to my own backyard and see the kitchen light is on, which means Mom is home.

She's going to want to hear everything, which is not going to happen. As I trudge to the door, I think that, if I could be honest with her, which I can't, this is what I'd say:

Mom, I'd say, *I have this hypothesis, about the first kiss and how it relates to true love, that I formulated because of Gigi and Harold's awesome love story, and your and Dad's less than stellar one.*

And tonight, for the first time in a long time, I wonder if I might be wrong.

I step inside, ready for her to hit me with a barrage of questions.

"No, Jack." She's on the phone with my father. I hear her in the dining room, and it doesn't sound good. It never is. "Are you serious?" she yells. Pause. "Well she's not going to want to be a bridesmaid. She doesn't even know the woman."

I pull the back door closed behind me. I assume this means that my father is getting married again, which isn't in itself a surprise. He got remarried after the divorce, and it lasted a whole two years.

"Well, that's great, just great," Mom says. "You need to ask her yourself. I don't want anything to do with this." Then there's silence, and then I hear her crying.

She comes into the kitchen, phone still in her hand.

"Oh no," she says when she sees me, her eyes all red and puffy. She sniffs. "Honey. Did you hear that?"

"Some," I say. She comes to me, and surrounds me with her arms. I love my mom so much. I love Dad, too, but together they aren't just inert, they're toxic.

I let her hold me for a few seconds and then pull away.

She sniffs again. "Do you want some cocoa?"

"No, thanks."

She fills the tea kettle anyway, and sets it on the hot plate to boil. "Did you have fun? You're home early." Her voice breaks again.

I can't stand this. "It's okay, Mom. Please don't cry."

Mom clears her throat and wipes her tears. "You had fun?"

"It was okay. Eli's knee started to hurt, so we left." Also, I experienced a little temporary insanity that this conversation is fixing, fast. "I'm tired, though." I watch her as she readies a cup for tea, tears still falling down her face.

This is what being with the wrong person does. This is the result.

"Are you okay?" I ask.

She smiles, but she's not okay. "Yes, of course, it's just

your father. He seems bent on making my life miserable…"

I can't do this tonight. I can't listen to her dump on Dad. "Mom, I'm really tired," I say. "You can tell me in the morning." I give her a kiss on her tearstained cheek and head to my room.

Marie meets me at the bottom of the stairs. I pick her up and hold her close.

That's what happens when you don't stick to reason, when you don't wait for the reaction. You cry your eyes out in a burned-out kitchen trying to make sense of your life.

That's not going to be me. Not ever.

I'll finish the lessons with Eli, and then that's it. As soon as I have my license everything will be back to normal. For now I just need to forget about that almost kiss in the water, and now in the garage, and move on. He's not getting a second chance. I can't give that to him, because the results of that kiss were clear. In science, a thing is or it isn't. And Eli Costas *isn't*.

Up in my room, I fall into bed. My phone buzzes and Marie pounces on it. It's Caleb, texting.

Game Thursday?

My brain is a jumble of messed up thoughts, I take a few deep breaths to clear it.

I'll give Caleb this: he doesn't waste time. I know what I have to do. With the sounds of my sniffling mom echoing through the house, I text him back.

I'd love to.

Chapter Eighteen

ELI

I can't sleep, the whole freaking night plays on an endless loop in my head. My knee hurts for real now, and I can't get comfortable. Surgery is a week off, the Monday of spring break. The doctors are hopeful, and the coach from CSU called and told me that there shouldn't be a problem holding a spot on the team once I'm cleared to play again. It's good incentive to work my ass off in rehab. I will be cleared to play if it kills me.

For now, Coach has me going to every practice, and assisting on JV. I'd rather be on the field, but it's better than nothing. At least it keeps my mind off possibly being too damaged to do well in college, or to get into a pro league. There's even been talk of making lacrosse an Olympic sport, which is something I've always wanted to do.

I thrash around in bed, as much as I can with my knee immobilized. There will be plenty of time to deal with all that shit later. Right now, I'm trying to work out what to do about my neighbor. Tonight was insane. Not in a bad way, completely. I mean, if my plan was to talk her out of her hypothesis by making her fall for me without a kiss, I'd say I definitely made progress.

Then I had to go and pour my heart out to her.

When we kiss again? Really?

NOT part of my plan? Asshat Tex asking her out in the laundry room.

Also not even remotely in the plan? I'm in love with her. What the actual fuck? I'm eighteen—I'm supposed to be playing the field, not falling in love.

Long story short, I'm in deep shit. She was supposed to fall for *me*, not the other way around. Now I can't stop thinking about her and I can't stop what I've started. We almost kissed, and she said, "Don't be sorry." I'm not sure what to think about that, except that maybe she's close to giving up on her theory. Maybe she just needs a little more convincing.

Or maybe I'm just a schmuck in love with a girl who can't love him back. Either way, it's full-court press time, and I've got a few ideas. When you're playing a game to win, you've got to assess the other team's weak spots and use them. I've known Nora a long time, and she's got a few I can capitalize on for sure. Like our history together. And pie. Definitely pie.

If I do this right, if I give it 100 percent like I do on the field, maybe we'll both win.

Or maybe I'll get my ass kicked and lose her forever.

•••

I'm in the empty hallway—well, me and a few other fellow students on crutches. We get out of class early because we're slow, or in danger of being further injured when our classmates blow out of the classroom doors, especially at the end of the day like it is now.

Nora has biology last period, so I head toward the science wing to catch her on her way out. I figured out where we're going for our next lesson, and it's fucking perfect.

The classroom door is propped open. Mr. Chaffee is sitting behind his desk, reading something while the rest of the class is talking among themselves.

I catch a glimpse of Nora's hair, or the back of it anyway. She's turned around and talking to Abby, and sitting at the table beside her is Tex.

Great.

I knew he was in this class, but do they really have to sit together? He leans toward her and says something, and they're both having a great time, and I want to bash his teeth in with my crutch.

"What was that, Mr. Costas?" Mr. Chaffee calls to me.

I may have made some sort of grunting noise just now, imagining taking a swing at Gray. Something came out of me that sounded pretty angry.

I shift on my crutches. "Nothing."

He gets up and walks toward the door. *NO, dude, stay, don't come over here.* He comes anyway, leans against the doorframe, and crosses his arms.

"Was that just you sounding your barbaric yawp to the universe?"

"What?"

He laughs and pats my shoulder. "Look it up," he says. "Are you waiting for Nora?"

I shrug and glance around his bulky body. Tex is still talking to her. "I'm her ride."

"Yeah, I know. Smart, that one. Going places."

"Yeah, I know." *Places you pushed her to go, asshole.*

"I was sorry to hear about your knee. You'll be missed on the field this season, that's for sure."

Thanks for bringing it up. "Yeah." I wish he'd go sit down. I'm trying to monitor the situation behind him. What if she says yes to him?

"Have you decided what you're doing next year?" Chaffee asks.

It's like a law when you're a high school senior that adults have to ask this question. It's so annoying. "State," I answer. Like I have a choice.

His jaw drops. "You're not serious?"

Um. Where's he going with this? "Yeah."

He squints and scratches at his lumberjack beard. "Come on, Costas. State? Your grades are good enough for better schools—how were your test scores?"

I crane my neck, trying to keep an eye on Tex. "Eh." I only took the ACT once, did good enough to get into State, which was the plan.

"I see. You're still going to apply though, right?" he presses. "North Florida, South Florida, Central Florida— good schools, all of them. Do you know what you want to major in?"

Another question adults are required to ask. "No idea."

He frowns. "Fortunately, you still have a time to figure that out. In the meantime, you need to apply," he says. "Those schools have decent lacrosse teams, too. I even went to school with one of the coaches at North Florida…"

I tune him out. Teachers get so excited about this shit. I hate to kill his buzz.

"Thanks, Mr. C, but I'm injured. I'm lucky that State is holding a place for me on the team for now. Plus, you know, school's not really my strong suit. You remember how I did in your class?"

He nods. He knows. "I remember you did well when you *felt* like it."

He's not wrong about that. The problem was I never felt

like it.

"Well, I hope you at least consider applying to more places. You just never know."

I try to see around him, see what Tex is up to. "Yeah, maybe. I don't want to get my hopes up."

"Eli, Eli, Eli," Chaffee says. "You're eighteen years old—your hopes are *supposed* to be up. If they get dashed to the ground, you need to grab them and get them up all over again! Do you understand me?"

I blink at him. "Um. Yeah, I guess." Dude needs to relax.

"Yeah?" he yells, really loud, and the whole class looks over.

"Yeah. Jesus, Mr. C, chill," I whisper, hoping he doesn't draw Nora's attention.

He looks convinced that I'm going to actually apply to these other places, and I don't hate that he thinks that I can, even if I'm not gonna. He steps back from the door. The bell is about to ring. I see Nora, and she sees me, and she smiles big. It might be my imagination, but she looks lit up inside, like she's glad I'm here. Tex is busy talking to Abby.

What did he say about getting my hopes up?

"Hey, Mr. C?" I call over the building pre-bell noise.

"Yeah?"

"Barbaric yawp? Walt Whitman, *Song of Myself.*" I have a fricking eighty-four in English.

He laughs. "Maybe you know what you ought to major in after all!"

The bell rings and Chaffee disappears behind the swarm of students rushing for the door.

"What was that?" Nora's still smiling as she exits the room, Abby at her side, Tex hovering behind them like an annoying buzzard. "What were you and Mr. C. talking about?"

"Oh, nothin', you know, he's a freak."

Tex edges up behind her. "Hey, Eli." He says to me. Dude is way too friendly. It would help a lot if he really was an asshole.

I lift my chin. "Caleb."

"What's up? You gonna be at practice tonight?"

"No, gonna lay off the knee tonight," I say. Coach asked me to assist at the JV game tomorrow night, the same one Tex asked Nora to in the laundry room. She hasn't mentioned whether she's going, and I haven't asked her, because I don't really want to know.

All I can think is she better not say yes. She hates organized sports. I've been playing since before we met, and she's only been to like three games, and only because I asked, and she complained the whole time. No way is she going to a game with Tex.

Hopefully that's not just me getting my hopes up.

I walk beside Nora, and it hits me again, the same feeling I had at O'Dell's. If I started to question it, I don't now. Love isn't too strong a word. "You ready?" I ask her, and notice Abby staring at me funny. Like she knows something's going on with me, even though that's impossible. Not that it matters. I have a plan, and time is wasting.

We're almost to the front doors and Tex manages to wrangle his way between me and Nora. "I don't mind giving you a ride home." His words hang over us like stink over cow shit.

Die, Tex. Die.

I cringe when she touches his arm.

"Thanks, Caleb, but I'm fine," she says. "Eli lives right next door. It's easy."

I check out Tex's face, which is almost always plastered with that annoying cowboy grin. Right this second, though, he's pouting like his favorite goat just died, and this makes me feel good.

When we get to MJ, finally rid of Abby and the asswipe, I hold out the keys to her.

"What?" she says, confused.

I jangle them in front of her. "You're driving."

Her forehead wrinkles up and she sputters out a nervous giggle. "No. I can't drive this thing."

This is gonna suck if she refuses to come with me. "Yeah you can. If you can drive your car, you can drive MJ."

"No, Eli, no." She tries to hand back the keys but I don't take them. "I need to practice in my car. I can't drive your truck."

I'm not taking no for an answer. "Come on, of course you can. This will be your final exam."

"Final?" The word drops out of her mouth, almost like she's sorry.

She's not as sorry as I am. "Yes, spring break is upon us, babe. I'm getting cut open, you've got an appointment at the DMV. It's time."

Her forehead wrinkles get even deeper. "Eli, A) I don't know how to drive this thing. And B), do not call me 'babe.'"

"Right, sorry. But you're wrong, you do know how to drive this 'thing'—it's no different from your car."

She shakes her head. "No. My car is not held together by duct tape."

"What?" I say with mock outrage. "You don't need to get nasty. You know I drive this truck all over. Mike's a beast. Trust me."

"Trust you?"

I feel the need to move closer to her, to remind her of what almost happened between us the other night. I don't want to freak her out, but I'm definitely in her personal space. "Yes. Trust me. I have a plan."

She lifts an eyebrow. "A plan?" The corner of her mouth turns up. In this moment, she's so sexy I want to give her the longest, deepest, lightning bolt-ish kiss ever. I feel like I could make that happen. Right now.

Now is not the right time, I remind myself, but I hope it comes. I need for it to come.

She grips the keys and walks to the passenger side. "Okay. I'll trust you this once." She helps me in and takes my crutches, throws them into the bed, and gets behind the wheel. Somehow, she manages to get MJ started on the first try.

I couldn't imagine anyone else driving MJ—Nora, though, she looks just right. "See," I tell her, "he already likes you better than me. Good job. Hey…" Crap. I almost forgot to ask. "You don't have anything going on tonight, do you?"

She backs out of my spot, like she's been doing it her whole life. "Why?"

"Just that we might be out a while."

"Where are we going?"

I beat a quick rhythm on the dashboard. "Not telling. Yes or no. Are you free?"

"I can always prepare for Science Olympiad."

This totally cracks me up. "So that's a hard yes, you're free. Olympic training doesn't count."

She smirks. "If you want me to drive, you have to tell me where we're going."

"Nope. You said you would trust me. I'll tell you exactly where to go. Don't worry. Just drive."

Instead she puts MJ in park and twists up her mouth. "I like knowing the plan."

Surprise, surprise. "You're such a control freak. Do you think, just this once, you can please, let me be in charge?"

"All right. Fine," she says. "I didn't realize I was so difficult."

"Well now you know. So just drive already. You're killing me."

Chapter Nineteen

By the time we get to the highway, I can't stand it anymore. I've kept my inner control freak at bay for long enough. "So *when* are you going to tell me where we're going?"

Eli throws up his hands. "That's enough! It's a surprise."

A wave of discomfort ripples through my stomach. I don't know why he's being so mysterious and I hope it doesn't have anything to do with what happened in the garage the other night. I need to forget about that, stick with my hypothesis. He's wearing the shirt today, though, the blue-green one, and his hair looks so good, messy and yet, perfect. Also, he's wearing the glasses, claiming his contacts are bugging him.

If we end up in another near-kiss situation, I don't know how I'll stop. I just know that I have to.

I inhale. "Well, I'm surprised." I switch lanes to avoid the semi that's barreling up behind me. "You're making me drive this truck to an undisclosed location on a busy highway." The sound of Michael Jordan going sixty-five miles an hour is so loud I have to shout to be heard. "I'd feel better if I knew there was pie involved."

"Don't worry," he yells. "This will be better than pie."

"Better than pie?" I am doubtful, and nervous.

On the way to this mystery location, we shout over MJ's clattering body about everything: school, what Mr. Chaffee said to him about applying to other colleges, about Ari and Gigi and his parents and my parents, about his dog, Chester, and Marie Curie. I love how we can talk about anything.

Of course, we don't say a word about O'Dell's garage, or the beach, or any of the weird moments we've been having lately.

I also don't tell him that I'm going to the JV game with Tex. Eli will understand. He knows my theory. In a few days I'll have my driver's license and things will change. We'll see a lot less of each other. He'll go to the parties without me. I'll probably kiss Tex and hope for a positive result.

I glance over at him. Maybe I should stop thinking about the hypothesis and enjoy this time with my best friend.

I've been driving forever through some lovely rush hour traffic, when Eli nudges my shoulder.

"It's the next exit."

"It's about time," I say, though I've done an excellent job driving us here, if I do say so. "Ocala?" I read what the exit says. "What's in Ocala?"

"You'll see," he says. "Not too much longer. Just keep driving, and go the speed limit."

I do what he says, and keep MJ up to speed. At the bottom of the off-ramp there's a big intersection and a billboard that says SILVER SPRINGS, with an arrow pointing right.

"There," he says. Turn there."

A rush of memory plows through me. All of a sudden I'm almost giddy. "Are we going where I think we're going?"

"Maybe. I don't know. Where do you think we're going?"

I giggle like the twelve-year-old I was the last time I came here. "I think we're going on a glass-bottom boat ride."

His lips are pressed together when I glance his way. "That would be a good guess."

"No way." I follow the billboards. "How late are they open?"

"Till six," he says. "I checked. We're good."

I pull into the lot and park MJ close to the entrance. It's a Wednesday in late February. There's almost no one here. "We needed to come all the way here for my final exam?" I ask. But I'm not annoyed. I'm thrilled.

He opens his door. "I just thought we could get out of town, too. Do something different. You *do* remember coming here?"

"Of course I do." I can't stop smiling. "That was a long time ago."

"You up for it again?"

I hand him the keys. "I just drove an hour on like three separate highways to get here. We're going on the boat, no matter what."

I set him up with his crutches and grab my wallet, but when we get inside, he won't let me pay the entrance fee.

Not this again. "Eli, I can pay."

He balances on one foot to dig for his wallet in his pocket. "Yeah, I know. So can I. It's not a lot of money."

No. This can't be a date. I clear my throat. "I'll pay you back."

He turns and slays me with his glare. "Nora, you don't have to pay me back, and don't make this about women's rights or whatever, okay? Just let me do this, because it makes me happy."

"Eli..."

He lowers his head so his mouth is next to my ear. "Just. Let. Me. Pay."

I step back, every nerve in my body on fire, and Eli pays

the man in the ticket booth. I'm watching the back of his wavy dark hair. I notice the way the muscles of his neck move when he does.

Is this a date? I'm not sure, but there are butterflies working overtime in my stomach, because definitely this is *something*.

"Here we go," he says, plowing through the gates on his crutches. "Let's do this."

I follow, amazed at how the park looks exactly as I remember it. The colors are maybe a little less vivid because it's winter, but they're still here, shiny bright-green leaves, and hibiscus blooming in pinks and oranges. Beautiful.

The boat launch looks the same, too, as do the boats. Green and white roofs. Windows all around the outside.

A man steps out onto the dock to greet us. "Afternoon, kids," he says when he takes our tickets. "I'm Captain Isaacs. Looks like you'll have the honor of being my last passengers today. Go ahead and have a seat, we've got plenty to choose from."

I'm speechless as I step on board. Eli expertly maneuvers on his crutches. It's just the two of us, and it feels like we've traveled back in time.

We sit toward the middle on the benches that surround the thick pane of glass on the bottom. There's a short wall to lean against and look over, which we do. Already, there are fish and plants beneath us in the shimmering water.

"Have you ridden with us before?" the captain asks.

"Six years ago," Eli answers.

"Excellent," he says. "You two related?"

"No!" Eli says. "No."

I smile at our captain. "We've been friends forever."

"Old friends are the best kind," Captain Isaacs says, as he steers the boat away from the dock.

We move slowly through the water, down the river, over rocks and a ton of fish. The sun going down makes sparkling patterns under the water, like glitter has been randomly sprinkled by some mermaid fairy. The captain narrates our trip, pointing out birds and all the different types of marine life.

"I need to bring Ari here," Eli says. "He'd love this."

"He's never been?"

"No. I've only been the one time. I never think about this place, you know?"

I think about it all the time, about our trip here. "Yeah." I don't *want* to, but I do.

The ride is amazing, but the best part comes when the boat moves over the mouth of one of the springs and the water turn from brownish to clear, crystal blue.

It takes my breath away.

The time we came, before, we were with Gigi, back when his parents were fighting a lot. I'm not sure what was going on, but I was terrified they'd get divorced. I hated the thought of Eli and Ari having to go through what I went through. I asked Gigi if we could do something fun with Eli, and she thought of this place. She was always good at coming up with the perfect solution—or she used to be.

That day the boat was crowded, and Eli and I were sitting at least this close, both of us staring down into the water, like we're doing now. I remember thinking the water was the exact same color of his eyes, so blue. Still is. Back then, I watched him and worried. He was so quiet, so focused on the bottom of that boat, and I got scared that he might end up disappearing into himself, like I had after the divorce. Dad was gone, and Mom was sad, and I was lost and so alone. He was the one who pulled me out again, starting on that first day, on the porch, with the blueberry pie.

I couldn't lose him, so I leaned forward on the boat, reached out my hand, inch by inch, desperate to hold him there, to keep him with me. I finally touched his back, and he didn't move. I felt his heart beating. Or maybe that was my own pulse, pumping so hard. He turned around and his eyes met mine. And I fell in love with him.

I'd forgotten that part of the story. That was where it started—my monumental crush that ended in disaster.

Fast forward to now, to Captain Isaacs going on about the amount of water produced by that spring, I'm tempted to reach out again and touch Eli. To somehow keep him here, even though he's wrong for me. Even though we're wrong for each other.

Instead, he's the one who reaches over, to where I'm holding the rail, and lays his hand on top of mine. Our eyes meet again and his shine bluer than the water, his dimple goes deeper than this spring.

I still love him.

It doesn't last long, his hand on mine. Maybe three seconds before he removes it and we go back to watching the water and listening to the tour. Captain Isaacs points out a school of catfish beneath us and tells us they're an invasive species. They're not supposed to be here.

I sit upright. Those innocent science-y words catapult me back to reality.

I'm not supposed to be here, either. I have an Eli problem, but the driver's license is supposed to take care of that.

My shoulders sag a little at the thought of losing him. His hand on mine felt so good. Not first kiss good, but still, *good*.

When we get back to the docks, Captain Isaacs shakes our hands and wishes us good luck, finishing with a wink. I wonder if thinks we're a couple, or going to be one. Couples who aren't chemically compatible need luck. Lots of it.

Is it possible, though? Could two people with enough love for each other make it, even without the explosive reaction?

No. Nope. That's dangerous thinking, and I can't go there.

Eli is my friend, and tomorrow I have a date with Caleb, and then I'll get my license and this will be over.

Enjoy this, I tell myself, *while it lasts.* We wander around, find the ice cream stand, and we each have vanilla. We got strawberries on it last time, but today it's colored sprinkles and it's all so delicious. We walk through the rest of the park. The animals and rides are all gone, but I can only think of his hand on mine. If he wants to hold it again, he can't because of the crutches.

That's probably a good thing because I'm not sure I could say no if he did. The sun is setting and the park is nearly empty. It's closing time. We make our way slowly to the parking lot, him because of his broken knee, me because I don't want this to end. He digs in his pocket and holds out his keys.

"Do I have to drive home?" I hear the whine in my voice. It is not attractive.

He doesn't seem to mind. "Ever heard of practice makes perfect?" He unlocks the passenger door. "The test is in two days."

I scrunch up my nose. "Don't you think I'm ready?"

He nods once. "You did a decent job."

"Decent?" I gasp, trying to hide my grin. "There wasn't a single broken bone."

He screws up his mouth, hops on his good leg, opens the door, and sweeps his arm across to signal I should get in. "Go ahead, hurry up, before I change my mind."

I stop in front of him, closer than I should be. I tilt my head. He squints in the setting sun. My heart beats fast. I try not to look at his mouth, tempting, like pie, pulling me in. "Thank you for this. I'm glad we came."

"Anytime."

His smile is sweet, and feels like more than a smile. It feels like an invitation. One I've never been more tempted to accept.

Chapter Twenty

ELI

The whole next day I'm trying not to pay attention to my brain, which is now constantly replaying yesterday and that boat ride, but I can't shut it down. The endless loop just goes faster.

I'm *really* confused.

The purpose of this plan of mine—disproving her hypothesis—I'm having a hard time remembering why I started in the first place. To keep her from getting her heart broken? To change her mind about leaving Edinburgh? Something about her not becoming a cat lady?

There on the boat, I thought, *yeah, she's totally rethinking the whole thing.* I touched her hand, and she looked at me, just like that day all those years ago. There I was again, drowning in those eyes, those big brown pools of quicksand that suck you in and eat you alive. I wanted to kiss her, bad, real bad, right there, with the captain probably watching our every move.

Will she give up the theory? Am I about to change her

mind?

I don't know. I just know that I want the answer to be yes.

In civics I sit next to Koviak and say nothing. He leans back in his chair and swats my arm. "What's wrong with you, dude?"

I point to my crutches, leaned up against the desk next to me. "My knee is jacked?"

"No," he says. "That's not what I'm talking about."

He waits.

I frown. "Nothing." *Everything.* I tap out a rhythm with my pencil on the table while Mr. Palumbo tries to pull up a YouTube video.

Koviak groans. "Don't even try to bullshit me. I've been watching you."

"What are you talking about?"

I know exactly what he's talking about.

He leans closer. "Come on. Why are you so afraid of her?" He lowers his voice, because the walls have ears at EHS, and so does Veronica, who sits right behind us.

"I'm not talking about this."

"Why the hell not? You're dumb as nails, Costas. She's hot, and she's available."

I level my eyes at him in warning.

He doesn't care. "Dude, look at you. You can't even stand me *talking* about her being hot and available. You look like you want to kill me."

I turn away from him. "You don't understand."

"What's to understand?" He moves in again. "You're a guy, she's a girl. Two plus two equals four, broseph. Go for it. And just so you know," he says, "I've been watching her, too. I see the way she looks at you. She's *always* looking at you."

She is?

"All right." Mr. Palumbo clears his throat. "Settle, class." He starts a boring video about the electoral college or some such shit. I hear none of it. I'm only thinking of what to do next. She's either close to dumping her stupid theory, or she's Nora Reid—stubborn as hell, and not likely to ever change her mind.

As the video drones on, I think of her, always her. That hair, that face, her body, and I ask a favor. Of God, I guess. I figure in the dark of the civics room, what do I have to lose? I start here:

If it's true that you created science and the laws that run the universe and all that shit that keeps us alive and not slamming into other things in the galaxy—can you help a dude out with a girl named Nora Reid? Like, can you give me a sign?

I can't wait to be with her in MJ, but on the way home from school, Nora is in a foul mood. She complains about her English essay—she got a ninety-four, which doesn't get a lot of sympathy from me—then says she got an email from Emory saying her scholarship application is being reviewed. She wonders out loud what that might mean. Is it good, is it bad? She wants to know.

I give her some nice, long, side-eye. "I'm pretty sure it just means your application is being reviewed...?"

"Right, thanks." she snaps at me, and doesn't say anything else. She's acting weird. Squirrelly.

When we get home, I park the truck and face her as she undoes her seat belt.

"Nor?"

"Yeah?" She's not paying attention. She's busy gathering up her backpack and a small box of brochures for the autism walk she's helping plan in April. She does more for my brother than I do. I'm a piece of shit compared to her.

"Hey, Nora?" I try again. Finally, she looks my way. "Are

we okay?"

Her nose scrunches. "Yeah, sure," she says.

I'm not buying it. Something is bugging her. I hope it's not me.

And also, I hope it is.

Samir the sophomore has the ball and I can almost see him working out the next part of the play in his mind. He's a good player. Really dirty, which in lacrosse talk means he's a killer. The problem is he's better in practice than he is in actual games. He gets in his own head, and that's the kiss of death on the field.

It's not an easy sport. You gotta have speed, agility, stamina. It's got the contact of football, requires the endurance of soccer, and the two-man game of basketball. You gotta be willing to share the glory, because it's a total team sport. Also, you have to be smart.

I suck at school, but lacrosse I get. You have to read the field, and you have to run the plays nonstop in your head. Samir will get there in time, I think, but for now I want to kick his ass. He passes the ball and it's picked up by the other team's midfielder.

"What the fuck are you doing?" I yell at the top of my lungs. The JV coach eyes me and I half smile an apology. Like Coach Johnston on varsity, he insists that we at least try to show some sportsmanship. Be gentlemen. Not cussing Neanderthals.

Easier said than done when they're playing like a bunch of morons.

We're well into the first quarter, and during a break in play, I scan the sidelines for certain people. I'm relieved. She's not here. Neither is Tex. Of course the first thing that comes to my sick mind is that they didn't even make it to the game because they're parked somewhere, making out and probably more. They'll be engaged in two weeks. I shake my head and force closed that disturbing image.

Some freshman whose name I can't remember botches another play. These assholes need more help than I can give them. Now Coach is yelling like a caveman from the sideline. I should pay attention, but I think of Nora. It's funny. She's a virgin. That's not even in question. She doesn't even care about that, as far as I know. That's not her priority. Her priority is...what?

Her priority is not ending up like her parents.

And so she waits, and waits. And kisses guys. And I wait, afraid she'll convince herself that some other guy is the one she's been waiting for.

I just need to convince her it's me. It's always been me.

I dig the end of one of my crutches into a divot in the field and wonder if I can make it happen.

How lucky would I be if she was mine? Well, not mine, because a person doesn't belong to another person. We could be each other's? She could be mine, and I could be hers. Damn that sounds perfect.

Play starts again, and I'm shouting directions to some of those freshmen who can't even seem to remember the easy plays. This one works, though, and I'm yelling at them and trying to run down the sidelines with my crutches. Samir makes a goal, and the team and the crowd go apeshit, and even though we're still down by one, there's a chance this crew might get their act together in time to win.

I turn toward the still-roaring spectators, heading for the Gatorade, when something catches my eye. A wave of auburn hair next to a tall, goofy-looking Texan in a lacrosse T-shirt.

Nora.

Nora Reid, who never comes to my games because she

"hates all organized sports" is in the stands. With him.

I crumple the paper cup in my hand, watching them as the crowd cheers on. I want to pick up this cooler and hurl it into the stands, knocking him into oblivion. Fuck. Fuck. Fuck. Why is she here with him? Because he asked her? Because she needs to kiss him?

She doesn't see me. She might not even know I'm here. She's too focused on him, staring up into his face. He's bending down, and she's smiling, and holy shit, are they gonna kiss? Right here? Right now?

No. No. No!

There's an elephant sitting on my chest. I can't breathe. The team must have done something good, because the crowd is going nuts again.

I turn away from them. Nameless freshman has just stolen the ball—I don't give a shit.

I won't turn and look at them again. I can't. There's this tingle in my throat, like you get when you're about to puke. I have this feeling that it just happened. They kissed. Lightning struck. I swear I can almost smell the scorched earth. Hypothesis proven.

My blood is running hot through my body, it's all going to my head which is about to explode.

Not that I believe in her damn theory. It's bullshit. But maybe if you want something bad enough, you can delude yourself into thinking that it's actually happened. All she needs to do is tell herself it was magic—and that's it.

I lose.

Like they've just thrown gasoline on my anger, I feel myself go up in flames. I need to leave.

I move down the sidelines carefully on my crutches.

"Coach, my knee's killing me," I tell him.

"Go home, Costas," he says. "Knee takes priority."

I don't look back. You know what? He can have her. I

hope they live happily ever fuckin' after.

I high-five Samir as he passes me on the sidelines, and then I head for the parking lot. I'm done. Done with my plan to change her mind. Done with whatever feelings I've had for her all these years. Time to shut that down.

I'm done trying to protect her from heartbreak, and a future as a lonely little medical-researching cat lady.

I'm done with worrying about her. I'm done loving her.

I'm done with Nora Reid.

We are done.

Chapter Twenty-One

Nora

I didn't know that Eli was going to be there, limping up and down the sidelines on those crutches.

I don't think he saw me and honestly, I didn't want him to. Not with Caleb. The thing is, Caleb's sweet and funny. He's not all about sports. He's smart, and wants to be an architect, and he doesn't just say that's what he wants to do— he's passionate about it.

Still, in spite of all that, our good conversation, and the fact he's super handsome, I had an impossible time keeping my mind on him and off of Eli.

Then something weird happened. Someone made a goal, or did something good, because the crowd went wild and I turned to Caleb. He was watching me. Not in a creepy way, but in an "I want to kiss you—now" way. Which was my cue, right? Put on my scientist hat, time to conduct my experiment. Kiss the boy. Wait for the reaction.

He seemed to be tuned in to what I was thinking, because

right then he lowered his face to mine, and…I pulled away! Completely out of kissing range.

Wait, wait, I almost said, *let's try this again.* Except I didn't want to say it. I didn't want to kiss him. It wasn't a choice. It was like a reflex—it wasn't up to me.

So I faced forward and cheered, because that's what everyone else was doing. It was a little awkward. Or maybe a lot awkward.

Now the game's over, and I am seriously having an out-of-body experience. Looking down on myself, I'm not sure who I am. I'm unrecognizable…and *still* scanning the crowd for Eli as we descend the bleachers. What's wrong with me?

Caleb and I make our way to the parking lot and I'm on the lookout for Michael Jordan. Caleb reaches out to take my hand. I freeze, stop in my tracks, and pull my hand out of his.

"Sorry." He's surprised and maybe disappointed. "I should have asked."

I stop looking for Eli, and remember who I'm on a date with. Oh my God, he's such a good guy. My inner Marie Curie (the actual woman, not the cat) is raging. *Kiss him, at the very least kiss him,* she says, in a thick French accent. *What if he is the one? The chemical reactant you've been searching for? The human you're made to be with? Don't be foolish!*

But I don't want to, Marie!

We reach his truck, giant and white and shiny, the total opposite of Eli's. He holds the passenger door open and peers down at me. "I'm glad you came," he says in that slow and sexy drawl, like he has no idea what's going on in my brain—which is total anarchy.

I laugh a crazy, machine-gun laugh. "Thanks for asking me."

"You know," he says, "you're not like the other girls I've met here."

"No?"

"No." His mouth curves up on one side. "You're not like any girl I've ever met *any*where."

I offer a weak smile. "Oh?"

"You're tough, and cute, and smart, and funny, and when I'm with you..." He rubs the fuzz of his buzz cut. "When I'm with you I feel weird."

"Weird?"

"Yeah, but in a very good way." He holds onto the door and leans close, so that I have no doubt what he plans to do next.

So what do I do? I jump into the cab of the truck, out of his trajectory. Again!

"Ready to go?" I chirp. Seriously, I sound demented. His confused face tells me that maybe he's rethinking the whole cute and smart and funny statement.

The ride home is a series of uncomfortable silences while I'm stuck in my head trying to figure out what's happening to me. Why I didn't kiss him. By the time he pulls into my driveway, I've come to no conclusions, and the first thing I think is MJ isn't here. Oh my God, I'm so relieved. In the worst way, for reasons I'm afraid to admit, I don't want Eli to know I went out with Caleb.

He turns off the engine and we sit in silence, another awkward slice of time between us. I'm fidgety, confused, and I want to get out.

"Should we maybe try this another time?" His voice is so smooth, like a less stoned Matthew McConaughey. He sounds totally relaxed, which I envy. "I get the feeling you're kinda distracted tonight."

I'm so distracted my brain can barely focus on his words. I want him gone before Eli gets home. I clamp my fingers together to still my hands. I don't know what to say. My brain is split in two, right side and left, debating each other. "Caleb..."

"Are you interested in me at all?" He says this so matter-of-factly that I know this isn't his first rodeo when it comes to rejection.

I'm desperate to organize my thoughts, put them into some sort of rational order before I speak. "No, it's not that," I say.

Of course it's that, it's exactly that. I am not interested, and I know what I have to do.

I tuck my hair behind my ears, and turn to him. "Caleb. You are amazing. All the good things. But...I'm sorry. I just can't."

He sighs. "You can't."

All of a sudden, I feel lighter, like something heavy has been lifted off of me. "I know it doesn't make sense, and you might think I'm a bad person. I mean, ask anyone. Cold. Harsh. Think I'm better than everyone else."

Caleb never loses eye contact with me, never stops smiling. "All right, now. That's bull. I think you're sweet."

"Me?" I say.

"Yeah, sweet and smart and opinionated," he says. "I like you."

Am I crazy, turning this guy down? I must be. "Thank you, Caleb."

"You sure you don't want to give it a little more time? I mean, we only just met."

I don't want to hurt him, I really don't—I've just never been surer of anything in my life. "I'm sorry. I can't explain it. It's just something I know."

Something I know that's changing everything.

He taps my arm. "I hope we're still gonna be friends. I could use a few."

I like this guy. *This* is a good guy. "I hope so, too, and so could I."

It would be decent of me to talk to him for a few more

minutes, but I can't. Something big has happened, and I need to get out of here. I open the door, lower myself down to the ground, and watch as Caleb drives away.

I don't know how I just did that—rejected the last age-appropriate male in Edinburgh I haven't kissed.

I only know I want to see Eli. Even if it's not right, or safe, or scientific. I need to talk to him, to somehow tell him what's happened to me and I have no idea what comes next. For now, though, I need to be near him. Hopefully I'll figure out the rest.

I glance over my shoulder at our house. I can't go in there and see the picture of Gigi and Harold when I might have just blown my whole hypothesis. So I go around the back, drop off my backpack, and sweep Marie Curie up into my arms. I know I can kill time with Ari and Mrs. Costas until he gets home. They'll keep me company so I don't obsess over the fact that I might have just made the biggest mistake of my life. Or done the best thing I'll ever do.

They'll distract me from the fact I've officially lost control.

I knock next door, and Ari answers, a cracker sandwich in his hand. Ari has a thing for crackers. He doesn't like bread at all, so everything is on crackers if he can help it.

"Hello," I say, holding Marie up in my hands. "Brought a visitor."

Eli and Ari have the same smile, the same dimple. Ari's goes just maybe a little bit deeper, especially when the cat is involved. He takes her from me as their dog, Chester, walks into the room, sniffs the air, and then plops down on the rug.

Mrs. Costas comes into the living room. "Oh, Nora, there you are. Do you know where Eli is?"

"No. I don't."

She pets Marie in Ari's arms. "He's not answering my texts."

"I saw him at the game, but he left before the end I think."

"*You* went to a lacrosse game?" she says. "Wow, how many pies did he promise to bake you?"

I don't get the joke. "Oh no, no pies. I just need to talk to him."

Ari giggles when Marie starts to scratch their sofa.

"Uh, no way, I don't think so little miss," Mrs. Costas picks Marie up and nuzzles the kitten against her cheek. "Well, why don't you come in and have a visit until he gets home? And speaking of pie…" She winks, hands the cat to Ari, and we all three walk through to the kitchen, where Mr. Costas stands, in his boxers.

"Michael, dammit, put some pants on!" she scolds him.

Ari inhales sharply. "Ooh, Mom, you said dammit."

"Sometimes it's the only word that works," she says.

"What? It's not like I'm hanging out of them," Mr. Costas mumbles. "Nora, I'll have you know I always wear tighty-whities under my boxers, for occasions such as this."

That makes me cringe. "Okay, thanks," I say, "that's probably more than I need to know."

"Don't pay any attention to him," Mrs. Costas says as she pulls a cream pie out of the refrigerator.

I gasp. That is not a Mermaid Diner pie.

Mr. Costas sits down with a mug and his phone. "Never let it be said I was indecent in front of the neighbors."

"Never, hon, now drop it, please," she says as she cuts a slice and passes it to me.

I love this family. I love Ari. I love their dog. Their home.

And their son? I can't believe this. Where has the real Nora gone? The rational thinker, the experimenter, the scientist, the believer in a universe that operates on strict laws and rules?

I dig my fork into this pie and realize that this is it: chaos theory, just like Eli said. The idea that some things are unpredictable. Like maybe love.

I don't believe that, or I didn't believe that, but these last two weeks I've spent with him, on all these driving lessons, in an attempt to *GET OVER HIM*—have changed me.

I taste the pie. Holy cow. It's the black bottom pie—like the Tick Tock, but not exactly. It's amazing. "Where did you get this?"

"Eli made it," she says, like he makes them every day.

I choke down my bite of pie. "Eli? Your son?"

She chuckles. "Didn't he tell you? He's taught himself how to make pies."

I swallow a forkful of the chocolatly, rich, deliciousness. "No, he didn't."

"He always loved helping your grandmother. I think he even went and talked to her, asked her for advice. I thought for sure he'd tell you."

"It was a surprise," Ari says, scooping up the chocolate from his pie onto a cracker, Marie mewing at his feet.

"Oh?" Mrs. Costas's eyes grow wide. "I'm sorry, I didn't know that. Well, I blew that one."

I stare at Ari. "Surprise? For who? Why?"

Ari chews, and with his mouth open, revealing half-eaten chocolate pie, he manages to get out four words. "Because he loves you."

I freeze. No one moves. Marie meows.

"Ari," Mrs. Costas says, her voice calm. "Of course Eli loves Nora. We all love Nora."

He picks up another cracker. "He wants to kiss her," he says like he's giving us the weather forecast.

"All right, Aristotle," Mr. Costas stands up. "That's enough of that."

"That's enough of that?" Ari repeats.

"Yes, that's enough of that." Mr. Costas takes another slice of pie. "But not enough of this."

"Michael," Mrs. Costas says. "Sweetie, don't you think one slice is enough?" She ignores what Ari just said, even though it's all I can think about. *Ari doesn't lie.*

"No, ma'am, I don't think one slice is enough." He walks to where she leans against the sink. "We have a son who doesn't give a rat's ass about school, but he can make a damn good pie. Life is short, woman. I'm going with the pie."

"Well." She pats his belly, which bulges more than it used to underneath his Def Leppard T-shirt. "We need you around for a few more years, so don't get carried away."

He leans forward and kisses her. "No way, I'm not going anywhere."

"Good." Mrs. Costas takes my plate and winks at me.

But I'm still stuck back on what Ari said. Eli made pie. For me.

There are butterflies doing cardio in my belly. My mind is like spinning like a ceiling fan on high. I can't think straight. I don't want to think straight.

I want him.

I want Eli.

Chapter Twenty-Two

Eli

I couldn't stay there, knowing they were up in the stands, knowing she was about to kiss him. So I limped my way off the field, threw my duffel in the back of MJ, and drove.

My knee, it's really hurting today, which makes everything else worse. As I drive I wish I could go away somewhere to college next year.

Where would I go to school if I could?

I've never been to any of the campuses Mr. Chaffee talked about, though some of them have good lacrosse programs like he said. I just can't imagine any coach will want an injured player. Plus my grades suck. It's too late. I'm stuck here.

My knee throbs like a bass line and I drive and drive. The more miles I can put between me and Nora, the better. I won't have to worry about her much longer anyway. She's getting her license tomorrow. I have surgery on Monday. I won't be driving her around anymore. I can spend the week recovering in more ways than one.

Thinking of her sends a flash of pain through my chest, like I might have ripped a muscle in my heart. But I know about injuries—they hurt the worst when they're fresh. I'll get over it.

Just a few weeks ago, I was fine knowing we'd only ever be friends. Then I saw that Emory email. That's what sent me off on this dumb quest. Then it just kinda went off the rails.

I don't even realize I'm getting off on the exit until the Tick Tock is in front of me. I've been here before without her. The day I had off from school, I went to the center and visited Gigi and asked her about pie making. She had Claudia look in a drawer and give me a small metal box. Inside were all her recipes. Then I stopped in here and talked the waitress, Fran, into sharing the black bottom pie recipe with me. I told her it was for a girl.

She winked. "The young lady who wasn't your date?"

I didn't answer, but she knew. I didn't care that she was right, because I had a solid plan to take her to Silver Springs and to make her pie, and the rest was supposed to have been history.

What an idiot I am.

I park and make my way inside. It's not crowded, so I take a seat at the bar and lean my crutches against it. I don't turn around to look at the booth where I sat with Nora and lectured her about my scientific theories. She didn't buy them then, and she doesn't today. It was just a desperate ploy to change her mind.

I tap a rhythm on the counter while I wait for a server. I don't see Fran anywhere. Fine. I don't need her asking me how the pie went over with Nora.

A waitress pushes through the swinging door to the kitchen—Charisse, according to uniform. She brings me the slice of blueberry I order and a cup of coffee. I did *not* order blueberry pie because I'm feeling sentimental about Nora. I ordered it because I like blueberry. Period. And I shouldn't have to justify that to anyone.

I douse the coffee with sugar and so much cream that it's barely recognizable, just like my pride.

I wish I didn't remember the first day we met so clearly. The details, like how the breeze blew her copper hair. She was like the Little Mermaid in real life, only with purple teeth.

I'm not sure I can eat any more. I push away the plate and consult the big clock that's been ticking since 1949. It's almost nine? I didn't realize how long I'd been driving aimlessly.

I pull the plate back. There's still plenty of time to wallow in pie.

"Want anything else?" Charisse asks when I'm done.

Yes, I want to say. *I want to not feel like total shit. Is that on the menu?*

"No, thanks." I pay the bill, leave a decent tip, grab my crutches, and take off.

Back inside MJ, I open my duffel bag, check my phone, which is overloaded with texts from Mom of the "where are you?" and "please check in" variety.

I dial home and Dad answers Mom's phone. "Where the hell are you?"

The muscles in my jaw clench. It's always this way with him. "Dad, I'm sorry, I threw my phone in my bag and forgot about it."

"Who are you with?" he barks in his gruff cop voice.

Shit, not tonight, Dad. "No one."

"You're alone?"

"Yes."

"Are you sober?"

I put the keys in the ignition. I don't need this right now.

"Yeah, I'm a hundred percent stone-cold sober."

He's quiet. "You know your mother worries."

I turn the key. MJ chugs once, then dies. I try again. Nothing.

"What the fuh—?" I say.

"Watch the mouth," he says. "Get your ass home now."

I try the key again. "I can't Dad. I think my truck's dead."

Let's just say Dad is not thrilled to have to drive all the way to the middle of nowhere to pick me up.

He slams his car door and strides over to where I'm leaning on MJ's bumper. "What the hell are you doing out here?"

That's what he opens with.

I feel numb and shrug at him. He doesn't really want an answer. He looks under the hood (like I already did).

"This doesn't look good."

Already knew that.

"Engine's seized up, I'm guessing."

My guess, too.

"I'll call a tow," he says. "Looks to me like it's DOA."

I slam my hand down on the hood, because yeah, I knew MJ was on his last leg, but today? *This* is the day he dies? It's like the universe has decided to drop trou and take a giant, cosmic dump on me.

I grab my duffel bag and a few other things. There isn't much. I grip the steering wheel. *You've been a good truck, Michael.* The tow truck arrives in record time. Dad talks to the driver, who he knows, because he knows everyone, even out here.

I get into Dad's Sentra. It's new and smells like plastic. No character. He stows my crutches in the backseat and takes off. I recline the seat and don't say a word.

After a few minutes, he clears his throat and I wait for the lecture to begin. "What were you doing out here anyway?" he asks. "Have you been to that place before?"

"Yep. Best pie in Florida."

He chuffs. "So you killed your car for pie?"

I inhale and adjust my knee. It's killing me. "I know it's not a good enough reason for you, but that's the whole story. Not drunk. Not high. Just getting pie. Your loser son just went to get pie."

"Okay." He merges onto the highway and we're on our way home. "You want to tell me what exactly makes you a 'loser'?"

We don't usually talk about stuff like this, but he asked for it. "What doesn't?"

He makes some grumbling noises. "No son of mine is a loser."

"Yeah, well, this one is. Can't get into college. Can't stay healthy. Women...total loser."

"All right, that's enough," he says. "What are you talking about?"

"Nothing," I mumble, eyes trained out the side window.

He's quiet for a long time, which is not like him, but I'm not complaining.

"You listen to me."

I spoke too soon. Here we go.

"First of all, State is a fine place to start."

Yeah, yeah. I've heard this all before. It's my fault for even bringing it up. Should have kept my mouth shut.

"In a few years, you'll transfer," he continues. "You know you haven't exactly put in the effort these last few years, so you'll dig your way out of it. Second, you know you can't rely on lacrosse, kid. There's always the potential for injury, but you *are* going to play in college if it kills me. You're too good and too young to stop now. And third, I don't know what woman you're talking about, specifically, so I'm going to go ahead and venture a guess."

"Dad." *Don't say it.*

"Nora?"

"No." I answer way too fast.

He huffs a breath. "Okay," he says. "She came over tonight, looking for you."

"I don't want to talk about her."

"Look, I don't know what's going on between you two, but I'm guessing it has something to do with that big white truck that dropped her off today. If you ask me..."

For the record, I didn't. Still, it's great to know the fucking tumbleweed brought her home.

"...you've been friends too long to throw it all away over a broken heart."

I can actually feel it, I think, cracking open. "She did not break my heart!" I yell. Like, loud.

"Okay," Dad says. "All right." He wisely says nothing else. I slump against the window and close my eyes.

Chapter Twenty-Three

NORA

Eli texted me last night that he wasn't coming to school today and I need to find another ride.

I texted back to ask what was wrong. I still hadn't had a chance to talk to him, MJ still wasn't in the driveway, and I was worried. He didn't answer, which isn't like him, but I figured his knee was hurting or something. He probably went to bed.

So now I have to wait until after school to see him. It's probably best, since I have no idea what I'm going to say. There are no rules for this kind of conversation.

I hate that. I like rules. No rules scare me. No control terrifies me.

Abby gives me a ride to school in her cute little blue bug.

I open the door and slide inside. "Hey, lady," she says. It doesn't take her long to get to the point. "So, how was it with Caleb last night? Is it true that everything's bigger in Texas?" She waggles her eyebrows.

"You crack yourself up, don't you?" I say. "For your information, not so good."

Her face falls. "No kidding?"

A flicker of guilt passes through me. I press my lips together, not wanting to talk about this. "He's really nice. It's just not going to work out."

"What's wrong with him? He's hot, smart, totally bone-able. What's the problem?" She takes a corner fast and the bug squeals. "Sorry. Or is the problem that he's just not 'neighborly' enough? You know what I'm sayin'?"

She laughs at her joke. For a really long time.

I wait for her to stop. "Are you done mocking me?"

"I am not mocking you. I'm just saying, there is not one girl at school who wouldn't jump at Eli, or jump *on* Eli, if they got the chance."

"Well I haven't stopped them."

She takes another corner too tight.

"Uh, yeah, you have," she says.

"What are you talking about? He dates other girls, and I have dated other guys."

"*Pfft*! So what if he's hooked up with other girls—and FYI, it's been a while. You, too, right? Tex was your first date in forever, yes? And don't give me that 'but we're best friends' bull. There's something between the two of you. Don't even try to deny it. You two should get together. I mean, it's about damn time."

I deny everything she says, although inside I hope she's right. "Okay. Okay," I say, hoping that she'll stop talking. I find myself wishing I was in Michael Jordan this morning. It's way too early for this.

After the last bell rings, I'm in bio cleaning up after the day's lab. I'm at the sink and freaking out about what happens next—which is me getting my license. I have the last appointment of the day at the DMV.

I finally told Mom, last night. Nothing like waiting until the last minute. She was surprised, and not exactly happy, and didn't like it when I told her I'd been practicing with Eli. She also didn't say no, and she'll be picking me up soon.

"Big plans for the break, Nora?" Mr. Chaffee asks from behind his desk. I turn off the sink and walk toward the front of the room, drying the graduated cylinder in my hand.

"Getting my license, hopefully," I say.

"Oh," he stammers. "That's…great."

Of course he knows about the accident. This town is way too small.

I frown. "Don't worry, I've gotten better. I've been practicing."

"Of course, of course, I'm sure." He waves off the concern. "Good luck. And thank you for washing those. It's not going to be the same around here when you graduate."

I put the last beaker away. "Don't worry, I'm sure you'll find another nerd to do your bidding."

He nods. "It's true, there does always seem to be one waiting in the wings, although I lucked out with you. You are going to be EHS's biggest success story. Not everyone makes it out of Florida. They get into state schools, yeah. Some good ones, hard to get into. Not Emory, though. That's rare." He seems so proud of me.

I avert my gaze. He'll be disappointed if he knows I might stay. "I can only go if I get some pretty big scholarships, you know."

He sits up. "You turned in the application?"

I nod. "Yeah."

"Your mom filled out the FAFSA?"

"Yeah."

He leans back in his chair. "Okay, good. You've got

excellent academics. Did you apply for work study?"

"Yes, but…"

"But what?"

More guilt. I rub my temple. "Nothing." I don't have the heart to tell him I'm just not sure about Emory. Whether I can leave Mom and Gigi.

We went to have dinner with her last week and it was just like when I was there with Eli. She was fine at the beginning, then couldn't remember who we were by the end. Mom was a wreck.

Of course, I also don't know how to leave Eli.

"I'm not buying that." He scratches his beard. "What's the problem?"

"The problem?" I might as well be honest with him. "Take your pick." My shoulders slump. "There seems to be an endless supply."

"You know," he says. "I know you're only eighteen, Nora, and I know you seniors get sick to death of us adults giving you advice about the future, but you and I go way back." He reclines in his chair and crosses his arms. "Listen to me when I tell you, you can go to State, even UF or FSU, and you'd be fine. I have a feeling you will thrive in Atlanta, though. They're studying things up there that, God, if I could, *I'd* go. Everything, or everyone, that might be keeping you here— you're not leaving them behind. The people who care about you, they'll be with you every step of the way, cheering you on." He chuckles. "And hey, you'll have your license. It's only a four-hour drive."

I grab my backpack and move toward his desk. "I know, it's just a big decision."

He sits up, his eyes kind like a dad's should be, like I hope my own father's would be, if I ever saw them. "Most of life's greatest adventures start with a big decision. You're a scientist, Ms. Reid. You have great instincts—that's like having a superpower. Use them, woman!"

I push my hair behind my ears. "Okay, Mr. C. I will."

"Promise?"

"Yes. I promise."

"Good. Godspeed, Nora Reid."

"Thanks, you, too."

Mom's waiting for me in front of the school. I walk around to the driver's side of her car and wait for her to get out. She opens the door slowly, her mouth in a straight line. I can see that her jaw is tensed. I know her angry face. She says nothing.

I touch her arm gently. "Mom, I'm sorry I didn't tell you about this sooner. I just didn't want you to worry. Trust me, though, I'm ready."

"Yes, I'm sure you are." Her words are clipped. She gets in the other side.

"Nora?" she says, before I pull away.

I wait, hoping she doesn't make this a thing. I know I should have told her, but I have to focus on the test. "Yes?"

"I thought we told each other everything."

I nod and grip the steering wheel. "Yeah—we do. Maybe not *everything*. The important things, for sure."

She crosses her arms and huffs. "Really?"

"Of course, Mom." I don't know what's going on with her, but she's making me nervous. She doesn't say anything else, so I drive. We don't have to be at the DMV for another hour, and I need to stay calm. I need to concentrate on the road. So I drive the few miles home, come to complete stops at all the stop signs, go no faster than two miles per hour above the speed limit. Put the car in park.

"See?" I say, smiling. "I'm ready."

She shakes her head, her mouth is set in a hard line. "You

didn't tell me that Eli was helping you practice driving. I'm not even sure that was legal. And now…"

"What?"

"Nora. I got on your email today."

I whirl around, and everything is clear. I know exactly where this is going. "Why?"

"Not to snoop." She holds up her hands. "I was looking for the car insurance information Dad sent you, because I need to find out how much that's all going to cost."

I wait for the rest, wishing I could accuse her of invading my privacy, when of course, she didn't. I'm just pissed off at myself. I should have told her.

"Nora?" Her voice is shaky. "Why is Emory University emailing you about a scholarship?"

I swallow hard. Except for my hypothesis, which she would never understand, Mom and I don't keep secrets. This is big.

"Did you apply there?"

My pulse thunders in my ears. I clear my throat. "Yeah, I did, and I didn't tell you because I didn't think I'd get in."

She gulps. I see pain in her eyes. "So you're thinking of going?"

"No. Well, I can't if they don't give me enough money. Even if they do, I don't know if I will. You need me here."

She laughs, only it's not a happy sound. Without a word she gets out, slams the door, and goes into the house. I follow her into the kitchen where she flings her purse on the table and crosses her arms.

It wasn't supposed to go down like this.

"Mom." I keep my voice calm. I didn't think she'd get this mad. "I didn't mean to keep it from you, I just… I didn't want to stress you out, and I guess part of it was I didn't want to get my hopes up. I knew that even if I did get in, and get money, it's still a huge decision to make. I know you need me."

She waves her arms wildly around. "Look at this kitchen!" She isn't quite yelling, what she's doing is worse—I think she's losing it. She walks to the burned-up wall and slaps it with her hand.

I say nothing; she's freaking me out.

I watch as she paces, hands on her hips, then plops into one of the chairs and starts to cry.

I go straight to her and put my arms around her. With all that she's done for me, I'm a little shit for even thinking of leaving. "Mom? Please. I won't go. I'll stay here. You need me." I hug her tighter, but she pushes me off of her and stands up.

A chill runs down my spine. I don't like this. "Mom?"

She wipes at her eyes and rubs her temples. "No! That's the problem. I'm always a mess, and you're always trying to fix things. Nora, *I* need to fix things. It's *my* job, not yours."

I step toward her, and she backs away. "Mom. That makes no sense. You're not a mess—and we fix things together."

"No." She sniffs. "It *does* make sense. Look, you got into Emory. That's one of the top schools for clinical research in the country. I looked it up!"

"So what? Mom, I can go later. It's not a big deal."

"Not a big deal?" she shouts. "Not a big deal?" She waves her arms again and then stops and points at me. "You are going to Emory. Even if they don't give you enough money. I'll work three jobs if I have to. I'll put the heat on your father. Don't you worry about a thing. You're going to college there."

My head hurts trying to follow what she's saying. "What if I don't want to?"

Her forehead wrinkles. "Why wouldn't you want to go?" Her voice reaches up an octave. "You love science; you've always loved science. Think about it, you can follow your passion, honey."

I am in shock; I did not see this coming. "I'd be leaving a lot behind," I say. As if on cue, Marie walks into the room and hops up onto the table. I pick her up and hold her close.

"No way." Mom smirks. "You're not using the cat as a reason not to become a disease-fighting scientist. I can take care of Marie, you know. And Gigi, and whatever else needs taking care of. I can handle it."

Tears well up in my eyes. "Gigi isn't getting any better."

She deflates. "No. She doesn't seem to be. Just hear me on this, sweetie, your grandmother would be furious if she found out that you turned down a chance to go to Emory. You know she would, and she'd murder me if I didn't do everything I could to make it happen."

I bite my bottom lip. Her insistence scares me. The whole conversation scares me. "I'm just not sure I want to go."

She sits down and gestures for me to do the same. "Why in the world not?"

I do sit, only on the edge of the chair, not letting myself get comfortable at all. I pet Marie to try and calm down. "I don't know? This is my home? I'd miss you. I'd miss...other things."

She's quiet, and when I look up, she's staring a hole in me. "Other things, my dear, can wait. If they're meant to be."

A chill runs through me. Honestly I'm feeling a little violated here. There's no way she can know how I feel about Eli. Is there?

A half hour later, I'm driving to the DMV. Mom seems okay now, but I'm a wreck. I'm glad that Emory is out in the open now, but I don't understand why nothing is ever easy.

I'm trying to relax, trying not to panic. What if I fail? What if I, holy cow...what if I hit the testing person? What if...

It takes me a whole ten minutes of "what ifs" to get to the driver's facility. We check in and wait for our appointment. I pull my hair back into a ponytail so it won't be a distraction.

You're ready, Eli said. Eli, who has disappeared into thin air. I never know if he's home with Michael Jordan in the repair shop. He isn't answering texts. I don't know what's happening. It's making me crazy.

Okay, Reid, stop thinking about him. About anything, and focus on this drive. This one drive. The stranger in the passenger seat coughs twice. Edinburgh is a small town, but I don't know this guy, even if he probably knows me by reputation. Also, I can smell his bad breath floating in the air. It's gross.

He starts the test and tells me what to do. I channel Eli. *All you have to do is stay in the lines and not hit the car in front of you.* This helps. I parallel park, do a three-point turn, circle the block a few times.

And I pass. With flying colors, as the stranger with the halitosis puts it.

Mom is thrilled. I am, too. My plan worked in one way—Eli doesn't need to drive me anymore—except I'm not even close to being free of him, and I don't want to be.

A tired-looking woman processes my paperwork and takes my picture. It's the worst picture ever, but apparently there are no retakes in DMV land. I'm still going to show Eli as soon as I can find him. Mom and I leave, license in hand, and I'm in the driver's seat, officially, legally. I start the engine.

Mom is beaming. "I'm so proud of you," she says, and asks if I want to stop for pie.

I don't. I want to see Eli. I need to see him, now. I go over the last few weeks in my mind. The moment at the beach. The garage. Silver Springs. Now the butterflies are at it again. In my stomach it's total chaos.

That's it, that's what I'll tell him. His theory was right. Mine was wrong. There might be a science to love, but it's not predictable. Mr. Chaffee said a good scientist follows her instincts, and my instinct tells me my hypothesis was wrong and Eli should get another chance. They also tell me that he's thinking the exact same thing. That he wants me as badly as I want him.

We pull into the driveway, and I'm out. "I'm going to talk to Eli," I say, my heart racing. I feel hot and a little dizzy and I don't care, nothing's going to stop me. I run over to their front door, ring the bell, and Ari answers.

"Hey, bud, how are you?" I ask him.

He smiles, like always. "Hey, Nora Reid, how are you?"

I hold up the license. "So good! Look! I can drive!"

"Oh," he says, and peeks over my shoulder. "Did you bring Marie?"

He loves that cat. "No, not this time. You can come see her later, though, okay? I need Eli. Is he home?"

Ari nods, puts his hands on his waist, elbows sticking straight out. "Yes." He rolls his eyes.

I step inside. "What?"

"Bad mood."

"Why's he in a bad mood?"

He curls up one corner of his mouth. "You know why."

I have no idea what he's talking about. "Well, whatever is bringing him down, this will make him feel better. Where is he?"

"Backyard." He moves away from me. "He's in a really baaaaad mood."

I'm not worried. I bound through the house, out to the yard where he's practicing throws on the bounce back, or trying to.

He's shirtless, wearing the glasses, and my whole body comes alive at the sight of him. My whole. Entire. Body. God. I'm not wrong about this. I step closer, but he has earbuds in and hasn't seen me.

The lacrosse shaft is in one hand and he's trying to balance on one crutch. It doesn't look like it's going well.

I run over, eager to help him and even more eager to be with him. "Eli!" Forget chemical reactions, forget lightning strikes and earthquakes. What I feel right now is bigger than all of those things.

This is magic. *This* is right.

He raises those eyes to me, bluer today than ever, but something is different.

"Hey. What's up?" He doesn't take out his earbuds, he just bends awkwardly with the crutch, trying to pick up a ball that he dropped. I move closer, pick up the ball for him, and hand it over, grinning.

His face is a blank. "You need something? I'm kind of busy." The ball drops out of his hand again and I reach for it.

"I'm fine. Leave it!" he yells.

I hold up my hands and step back. "Okay, fine. Wow. Ari wasn't kidding, you are in a bad mood."

His upper lip curls into a snarl. "So? I can be in a bad mood. What do you want, Nora?"

I don't know why he's acting like this, and I don't care. I can change his mood. I know I can. I take a step toward him, and another. God he's handsome. Why did I ever say no to him?

It ends now, the saying no. Every step I take forward feels like a step toward something new. Something chaotic, maybe. Something unpredictable, for sure, but also something good. I'm ready to set aside everything I thought was true about love and what makes it work. Seeing him, now, even grouchy, I know it'll be worth it.

My hypothesis was wrong. Every step I take toward him is the right step.

My heart is beating fast, but steady. "I got it!" I hold out my license and throw my arms around him, ready to tell him everything.

Chapter Twenty-Four

ELI

Her arms are around me and she squeals. "I got it!" She holds out the license for me to take, a huge smile on her face.

I nod and don't reach for it, maintaining the disinterested look on my face. "Great. I'm happy for you, but like I said, I'm busy." It's not true. I'm not busy at all, and it's hard to be such a dick to her. It needs to be done, though. I need to put some distance between us.

Her forehead crinkles up. "Eli?" She's finally catching on. This isn't just Eli being grumpy. This is Eli, changed. I don't say anything. I don't want to talk to her. It hurts to be this close to her.

I try to turn on my one crutch and almost fall. She steps close and takes my arm to steady me. I make the mistake of making eye contact. Now I'm screwed.

The smile flickers again on her lips. "Listen to me," she says.

She's got me hypnotized. Must look away. Can't. "What?"

"These last few weeks. With you."

You mean the last few weeks when I fell in love with you? Yes, I'm aware of them. "Yeah?"

Her face is turning red. She's blushing. "Yeah," she says. "You have to admit. There have been…" She scrunches up her nose, like she does when she's thinking.

My breath catches in my chest. She's still holding my arm. "What?"

Her head tilts toward me. "Um. Moments? Things have happened. Right?"

"Moments?" There. I break her gaze, pull myself out of her grip. "What are you talking about, Nora?"

She moves closer. "I've been thinking. About. Well, about my hypothesis, I guess?"

This makes me laugh. I scratch my head. "Oh, good, let's talk about the hypothesis! That's just what I want to do." I hop toward the garage where my other crutch leans.

"Eli…" She follows. "No. I mean I've been thinking about what you said. About chaos theory."

"What does that mean?"

She beats me to the other crutch and hands it to me. I hate that she's helping me. I hate that she's so beautiful.

She cranes her neck, trying to meet my eyes again. I won't let it happen. "It means—well, the other night, at Silver Springs…"

I let out an exasperated puff of air. "Yeah. That was a stupid idea. To go there."

Her hand reaches out, she touches my arm. Those fingers sear my skin and I swallow hard and there they are, her eyes.

Her mouth curves up, just a little. "No. It wasn't stupid." Her voice is so soft. "It was perfect. It made me think, Eli. About us." She clears her throat. "I was thinking maybe we could try again."

Now she's the one to look away, tucking that crazy hair

behind one ear. I almost reach up and touch it. *Wake up, Eli.*

"Us?" I sneer. "What *us*?"

She takes a small step backward. Which is good. I need this space. I shake my head to clear it.

Is she saying she wants there to be an us?

"Are you saying you're gonna let me kiss you again?" I ask. "Because of the last few weeks?"

She looks surprised that I'm calling her out. "Eli. I..."

Meanwhile, I'm stumbling through a minefield of anger and confusion, and there are mines exploding all around me. She wants us to kiss? Is she insane? No fucking way—I saw what I saw.

"That's great," I say. "That's just awesome. We're having these moments, and you're feeling these feelings, and you loved Silver Springs so much, but you still—you still go to the game with *him*?"

Her eyes flash—aha, didn't see that one coming. "No. That's not what. I mean, I didn't want to go."

My body quakes, my blood is boiling in my skin. "No, see, that's the thing. All the years I've known you, you've never done anything you didn't want to do. You make the rules, Nora. You always have."

Her face turns red. "Eli, no. I just went with him because..."

"Because you had to be sure that Tex wasn't the guy you've been looking for? No, I understand. You covered all your bases. Nice."

Her body deflates, just a little. No way can she explain this away, because I just hit the nail on the head. "I've got stuff to do, Nora." I drop the extra crutch and grab the lacrosse shaft, drop the ball in the net, and turn away.

"Eli...please."

I lift the shaft up over my shoulder, line up my shot. She's still there and I want her gone. "I *said* I'm *busy*." I glare at her, then at the bounce back. I aim then throw. Not even close, which feels really symbolic right now.

"But Caleb and I—" She touches my arm and I flinch.

"Nope. No. Don't say his name, okay?"

"Eli," she says. Then, after a long pause, "I want another chance."

My muscles freeze, my brain stalls. I straighten my spine and let myself look at her. She's about to cry. I don't care. As long as there are guys out there that she hasn't kissed, I'm not safe. I can't trust her.

I scowl. This is like playing in a big game, when the score is tied and the gloves come off. There's no way I'm letting my defenses down now.

It's time to go for the jugular.

"I knew I could do it!" I blurt out.

She bites her bottom lip. She's worried. I know so many of her faces. I know her better than I know myself. "Do what?" she asks.

I make myself keep eye contact. She's not getting off easy. "I knew I could prove that the kiss has nothing to do with it."

"What are you talking about?" Her voice is almost inaudible. I hope she doesn't cry.

Wait. No. I hope she does.

"What, you think all these 'moments' over the last few weeks, you think they were an accident?"

"I don't understand."

I put on my biggest douchebag game face—I know exactly how to do it—curled lip, looking down my nose—talking serious smack. "Yeah, the beach. The garage. The boat. That was my plan. To make you fall for me, to prove that even with a crap first kiss, you could fall for someone, even me. No lightning, or thunder, no fucking earthquake. Just me. And it worked." Cue total asshole sneer.

She scrunches up her nose like she smells something bad.

The tears are ready to drop. "Why would you do that? You're my best friend."

Tears don't stop me, though. The pleading in her voice doesn't stop me. "I am, and I didn't want you to end up miserable and alone. So I changed your mind, right? You're willing to give me another chance? What, did Tex kiss you and it sucked? Probably made the decision to forget your theory a little easier."

"No!" Her voice cracks. "That's not what happened. I didn't even kiss him."

She's hard to look at, with the tears now rolling down her face. I dip down and pick up my other crutch. "Good, so you kept him in your back pocket. What a relief. I'd hate to think you missed out on the perfect guy."

I turn away and stumble toward the back door. I'm done with this—done with her.

She says nothing, but I hear her crying. I'm hobbling faster now. I've got to get inside; I can't stand making Nora sad. As mad as I am, that hasn't changed. I reach for the doorknob and she lets out a heaving sob, which is more than I can take. When I turn around again, she's a blur across the driveway. Like a bolt of lightning, she's there and gone.

The next day, Saturday, something begins to make itself clear to me: mostly, that I'm a giant wang. Even though I had to be. I was protecting myself. Even with her telling me she didn't kiss Tex, she would have rejected me again, and it was hard enough the first time.

At least I'm man enough to admit I lost my shit with her. I didn't know what I was saying, and didn't believe what she was saying. She wanted another chance. There's no way.

I'm glad it's spring break, and that I can sit in the house

and do nothing. The surgery is on Monday, and it's an outpatient thing, so I'll be home that afternoon, hopefully mellowed out on some major pain meds, and then it's back to rehab the next day. Rehab sucks so bad. The only good thing is they don't let you sit around feeling sorry for yourself.

Neither does Mom, who comes into the living room with a basket full of clean laundry and dumps it at my feet. She has no respect for the fact that Ari and I are on vacation, and we're currently busy lying around in our underwear watching old episodes of *SpongeBob* on Netflix.

"Fold, boys!" she orders.

It's a full five minutes before I move myself to a sitting position and grab a towel. "Come on," I say to Ari, who has his knees pulled up to his chin, mesmerized by that yellow sponge. "Help me."

He laughs at something that happens on screen, then reaches over half assedly and grabs a washcloth.

For the most part he just sits there, not taking his eyes off the TV. "Hey. Fold!"

Suddenly, he turns my way, and like he's telling me what's for dinner, says, "You made Nora sad."

I frown. "What the heck are you talking about?"

"You made her very sad. You yelled at her. I heard you."

I stop and gauge how upset he might be. He doesn't like yelling. I didn't realize he heard us yesterday. I wish he hadn't.

The towel I'm folding is a mess, so I start again. "Ari. She's fine." But who am I trying to convince—my brother or myself?

"No." He turns back to *SpongeBob*, crumpling the washcloth into a ball. "She's sad."

"Well, there's nothing I can do about that."

His head snaps back to me. "Yes there is. You can get married."

I snort. "To Nora? Why would I do that?"

He eyes me, offended. "You love her."

"Ari...it doesn't work that way."

"It does. Mom said."

"Okay, let me tell you something, little brother."

He pulls his knees tighter under his chin, waiting for me to speak.

I lower my voice. "Mom doesn't know everything."

"She said that when people love each other they get married, and you love Nora."

I start folding the towel again, third time now. "Right. Okay. Look, Ari, that's enough. I know you think Nora is perfect, but she—"

"She loves you, too."

I press my lips together, not sure what to say. I don't want to upset him. "No. She doesn't."

"Yes she does."

"No she doesn't."

"Yes she does."

I know when I'm fighting a losing battle. "You gonna fold that washcloth or marry it?"

He turns the fabric around in his hands, then looks at me, totally confused. "You can't marry a towel."

"And I can't marry Nora. Got it?"

He nods and goes back to the show. It's the episode where SpongeBob goes to boating school. Hilarious.

If only I could stop thinking about what I did to Nora, I might actually enjoy it.

One episode later, all the laundry is folded, no thanks to my brother. I grab the pile of dish towels and put them away. The kitchen is quiet. Mom is upstairs, Dad's at work, Ari's in front of the TV.

I look out the window above the sink and stare at her house. Not long enough to get caught. I don't know if she's home.

I don't care. I did the right thing. Probably.

I glance around the kitchen. There's a bag of Granny Smith apples on the counter that are starting to get soft. There's no one around to bother me, so I do the only thing a gimpy attackman who might have just made the biggest mistake of his life can do: I go get Gigi's recipes and make a fucking pie.

Chapter Twenty-Five

NORA

Friday night I was so mad at Eli I couldn't see. Blind. Blind with rage. When I went back into the house, Mom knew something was wrong, but how could I explain? *I* wasn't even sure what happened, and I'm still not sure I want to know.

It was like he was accusing me of doing something wrong, when literally all I did was fall for him. Hard. Too hard to get up again easily.

So I didn't. I stayed in bed most of the day on Saturday. Somewhere between episodes of *Gilmore Girls* and napping with Marie Curie, I realize:

Eli didn't disprove my hypothesis, he totally proved it. We had a bad first kiss, and he was and is still totally wrong for me, which means my theory is sound. Yes, okay, I let myself fall for him. I let myself forget the science. I did that. The rest was all him. He said it himself—these last few weeks were all about teaching me some sort of sick lesson. I didn't stand a chance.

I just wonder what he thought was going to happen next. He was only pretending to care about me.

Unless he wasn't…?

I don't believe that, though. Not as cruel as he was to me in his backyard.

Clearly, he doesn't care, and he certainly doesn't love me. In fact, now we're not even friends.

On Sunday I know I need to get up. No more wallowing. I'm an intelligent woman with a bright future, even if it is at Citrus State. I have homework to do, the Science Olympiad to study for. Cat poop to scoop.

My life is nonstop adventure and fun.

Abby texts me and asks what I'm doing Thursday. Apparently there's a bonfire at the beach. She's grounded, and she really wants to go, which I now know is Abby code for, *I need to tell my parents I'm at your house.*

At least she invited me this time.

There's still no word from Emory, which isn't bad news— yet. They start handing out money in late March, although I'm trying to not get excited, because I probably won't get enough. If I don't, I'm staying here. There's *no way* I'm going to watch Mom sink into debt because she thinks that's where I should go. Money from Dad is not realistic. I love him, but he's the biggest cheapskate ever. State is cheap, and I can live at home. Why would I want to do anything different?

Ugh. I roll out of bed and go to the window. It's bright and sunny and the opposite of my mood.

What I need right now is Gigi.

All my life, she's helped me see past the terrible things and focus on the big picture. I just hope she remembers me.

Mom is at her plaque scraper's study group today, so I

get in the car by myself for the first time. I'm surprisingly relaxed, or maybe I'm completely lying to myself. I forbid myself to turn my head toward the Costases's house as I back down the driveway. I don't want him to think I care what's going on over there.

Every time I think of what happened, it's like being hit by a steamroller. Flattened, all the life gone out of me.

The drive goes well. I only miss the entrance once, and I don't almost hit any cats. The center is buzzing with activity, and the smell isn't too bad today. I think it's being masked a little by the strong odor of maple syrup, probably from breakfast.

Claudia opens Gigi's door when I knock. "Well, hello there," she says. "It's good to see you."

I feel somewhere else, not on the planet. I force myself to land and smile at her. "You, too."

She peeks out the door before she closes it. "No Eli today?"

I stiffen hearing his name. "No. Just me."

"Well okay, that's fine by us, right, Maggie? Look who's here."

Gigi is in her chair, knitting. She looks up and her eyes brighten. "Nora." She waves me in.

Thank God. She knows me.

Claudia winks. "It's a pretty good day today."

I go straight to my grandmother. She lifts her arms and gives me a tight squeeze. It feels so good and I let it sink in, the feel of her love surrounding me, one of my favorite things in the world. I need it so badly right now.

She points to the chair beside her. "Have a seat and tell me what's wrong. You look like someone just kicked your dog."

She sounds strong today, so much like her old self. I wrap that around me, too.

"If you ladies don't mind," Claudia interrupts, "I think I'll take a little break. All right with you, Maggie?"

Gigi huffs. "Of course it is. I don't need a babysitter!"

Claudia chuckles and makes her way to the door. "No, you most certainly do not."

"So tell me what's wrong." Gigi waits.

I swallow hard. I didn't come here to ruin Gigi's day, but if I could get some of her advice, that would be amazing. But where do I start? I lean forward on the table, and prop my chin in my hand. "Everything?"

"Oh my. That's a lot of things."

My mind is overrun with things to say. I inhale, ready to let it all out. "Everything. Everyone. I don't know." I flip the pages of a magazine on the table, not even looking at it.

"Where's the boy today?"

"Eli?" It hurts to say his name.

Her eyes dim for a second. "Yes, of course, Eli." She scans my face, knowing that she forgot something she should have remembered.

I swallow. "Not coming today. Or ever again, probably, at least with me."

"Ahhh. So *he's* the problem."

I don't confirm or deny.

"What happened?"

Flipping pages manically, I blow out a breath. "He did something terrible."

Gigi reaches out and touches my arm, stilling me instantly. "How terrible?"

Somewhere in my chest, I can feel my heart crumble just a little more. "So bad we can't be friends anymore."

Both her eyebrows lift. "That doesn't sound like him." She *tsks*. "He must have changed. He's always seemed like such a nice boy." She wrinkles up her nose. "Didn't he make you a pie?"

My mind goes back to the Costases's kitchen, and the surprise pie Eli made. "What?"

She pauses. "Yes. I remember he came here. He asked me how to make pie. Didn't he?"

It's hard, seeing her confused. "I think he must have."

It's like a memory is dancing around her and she's trying to catch it. "Yes, he did," she says, stronger. "He said he was going to make a pie for you. Because there was some other boy trying to woo you."

I blink. "He said 'woo'?"

"I don't remember." She moves her hand off my arm and sits back. "I told him to make sure his butter was cold, you know, because that's the key to a perfect crust."

"Really?"

She smiles. "Oh yes, I gave him my recipes. He didn't give you a pie?"

Another chunk of my heart falls off. I'm like a melting glacier. "No, he made a pie. But he didn't give it to me. He was tricking me because he thinks my ideas are stupid. Because he doesn't think I should wait to find what you had with Harold."

Again, confusion spreads across her face. "Harold?"

"Yes. Harold? Grandpa. You had that magic first kiss with him, and you knew he was the one."

She holds her hand up to her lips, like she can still feel it. "Yes, I did."

"Yes!" I say, so loud it startles her. "I mean, yes, that's exactly what I'm waiting for, what you always said—it's like a chemical reaction, it either happens or it doesn't, and it happened for you. You were meant to be. That's all I want— that kiss, like you had with Grandpa, the kiss that will tell me I'm with the right person. So that I'll never…"

"Never what, sweetheart?"

I lift a shoulder. "Get my heart broken? End up like Mom

and Dad? Divorced, depressed, lonely? If Mom had waited for that reaction...or Dad had..."

She sits up taller in her recliner. "Oh, pooh! If they had waited for some silly reaction, you wouldn't be here!"

Silly reaction?

"I'm sorry, dear. It doesn't work that way. Love isn't a reaction. Reactions fizzle out."

She pokes at my arm to make sure she has my attention.

"Well don't they? I don't think that love is 'there' or 'not there'—it's not that simple. The first time I kissed my Harold, yes, it was full of passion, and magic, yes it was. And then we got married after two weeks! How stupid was that?"

She chuckles, remembering.

This conversation is not going according to plan. I feel low-key nauseated. "You always said you were happy."

"Well of course we were happy, and then we weren't, and then we were again. Don't think just because we were married for forty years he didn't ever break my heart. He did, and I broke his." She pauses, remembering. "There were a few times I wasn't even sure we'd make it."

My own breaking heart is pounding fast. She must be remembering wrong. I need her to tell me I'm right, that there is a science to finding true love. I need her to tell me that the first kiss is everything. "But you *did* make it," I say. "Because he was the right person for you. You knew it from the beginning, because of the kiss. You said it was like a lightning strike. Or an earthquake. You *knew*."

My grandmother watches me, full of love, no sign of a glitchy memory, and takes my hand. "The kiss, the kiss, the kiss, Nora, Nora, my dearest. I do think that some people are meant to be together, and maybe you can know it. For me, it was like an earthquake, for you it could be different. Your 'earthquake' might be a touch, or a glance. It might be a terrible first kiss, followed by a magnificent second kiss. It might be a friend who makes you pie."

Her eyes light up and she winks at me.

My mouth goes dry. She knows. What did he say to her?

"Well I was ready, Gigi," I blurt out and try to control my quivering bottom lip. "I was going to give him another chance. Then…" I can't help it. I start crying.

"Oh no, oh dear, oh no. Come here," Gigi says.

I don't want to cry. Crying is a waste of time, but I can't seem to stop, so I go to her. I kneel in front of her recliner and she puts her arms around me.

"Oh, oh, come now."

I lay my head in her lap, sobbing.

She smoothes my hair with her small, frail hand. "You know the best thing about love?"

I sniff. "No."

She seems lost in a memory, somewhere far away. "It's unpredictable. That's what makes it such a miracle. So wonderful. It can't be defined, or proven. It's too big for that. Don't try to make it small. And don't you dare let it pass you by." She keeps brushing back my hair, humming a song I've never heard. "I've always liked your hair down like this," she says. "It suits you."

I let myself absorb her words. I feel her touch, and soon, I'm not crying anymore.

When Claudia comes back, Gigi is asleep and I'm still at her feet. She helps me up, and Gigi doesn't stir.

I cover her with a blanket from her bed and bend down to her ear. "I'll see you next time," I whisper, then kiss her gently on the top of her head.

I love her so much, and even though I'm not sure I can get past what Eli's done, I think I see her point.

Love—family, or romantic, or whatever—is big. Maybe too big to be quantified by an experiment, or explained by science.

Maybe it was wrong to even try.

Chapter Twenty-Six

I'm on some heavy painkillers. Trippy. Knee surgery was a success. Woo-hoo! I think that's what they said, anyway. I was so out of it I can't remember. Something about me having bionic knees. Something about being cleared to play by the time I get to college. No problem.

Damn. I'm going to college. I lie in my bed, high as a kite, thinking about what that means. First, no more Edinburgh High School. Which is fine. I had an okay time there, but I won't miss it much as long as I get to keep playing lacrosse. Second, I don't have a clue what I'm gonna do with my life. Going pro sounds fun, unless I'm not good enough. If I'm not, then what am I gonna do? I have no idea. What's wrong with me that I have zero plans for the future? Probably 'cause I wet the bed until I was six.

Heh. It's like I'm in therapy and the therapist is me!

I laugh and laugh.

I gotta pee.

"Don't wet the bed, Costas," I say. Out loud. I think I said it out loud, anyway.

The worst thing about going to college, to State, anyway, is this: no Nora. Because she's going to Emory. I know she is. You know she is. We all know she is. After what I said to her, who can blame her? Not to imply that's why she's going. The real reason is: she's so fucking smart. She'll probably discover a cure for cancer first semester. Find the cure for—what? Something else really bad—second semester. What the hell am I gonna do without her?

These pills, they numb all sorts of pain. Not all of it, though. Not even close. I need some Nora-quil. That's what I need.

I laugh about that for a really long time.

I should have kissed her. I should have taken her in my arms, leaned in, and said, *fuck it, I don't care if this is the worst kiss in the history of kissing, you can dump me again and again and again and I'll kiss you again and again. It would be worth it!*

Mom comes into my room without knocking, Ari at her side. "Honey, we brought a snack," she says. She's got a glass of water, and Ari's holding a plate of something. I can't tell what. They're both kind of swaying in the doorway. I close my eyes.

"You ready to eat something?" Mom asks.

"Uhhh." I groan. "No."

My stomach's been a wreck since I woke up from the surgery.

"I gotta pee."

"Okay, honey." Mom sounds worried. "Let's get you up."

Between the three of us, I get into the bathroom and do my business without passing out. I'm starting to come back to earth a little bit.

Mom props the pillows behind my head. "You want to

watch some TV?"

"What do ya say, Ari?" Mom won't let him sit on my bed, just in case my knee gets knocked around. He stiffens up, on the verge of getting upset. "*SpongeBob*?" I ask.

He relaxes some. "Yes." He sounds relieved and grabs the remote while pulling up the desk chair. Mom leaves us alone while he finds the boating school episode, of course. It's his favorite.

It's also ironic because it makes me think of driving school, and Nora. Really, though, on these drugs, what *doesn't* make me think of Nora?

"You doin' okay?" I ask my brother.

He's mesmerized by *SpongeBob* and doesn't respond.

"Yo! Ari?"

He turns to me. "You're gonna die, Eli."

"No way, dude, not ever."

He tilts his head, considering what I've said for a whole ten seconds. "Okay." He still holds the plate in his hand, it's a slice of pie and he's eating it. "Where'd that come from?"

"Nora."

"She brought it?" It's black bottom, from the Tick Tock, I can tell.

He takes another bite, and chocolate smears on his upper lip. "No, her mom."

I'm confused and scratch my chin. "So her mom brought it."

He nods. "Yeah."

I check my phone, even though I'm still not exactly seeing straight. Texts from most of the team, wanting to know if I'll live. Koviak, who's still begging me to come to the bonfire on Thursday. Nothing from Nora.

Even if her mom brought it over, she probably suggested it, so it's from her. Right? "Hey, yo." I focus on Ari again. "That was supposed to be for me. Give me some."

He grudgingly passes the plate, where there's only about a third of the slice left. I don't care. She brought me pie again. Somewhere in my painkiller-numb brain, knowing this makes me feel a whole lot better.

I wake up after a night of drug-induced, weird-ass dreams. The weirdest? Me, in full lacrosse gear, swimming in the ocean. I hear Nora calling out for me, and I can't find her. I frantically flap through the water, trying to save her. When I find her, she's already on shore, all like "I don't need your help." Tex is standing beside her, in hockey gear and a cowboy hat, which he tips to me.

I'm pissed the whole morning, and then I have to go to rehab, so things don't get better. I still work hard for the physical therapist. It hurts bad, but I gotta get used to it. This injury was worse than the last time. Recovery's going to take longer, and I gotta push hard. If I don't, I won't get to play for State, or maybe ever again. Intramurals maybe, or when I'm old and fat on some amateur league trying to relive my youth.

That afternoon, someone knocks on my bedroom door. Dad doesn't wait for an answer, though—he just plows into my room.

"Eli!" he shouts, and I wait for him to yell at me for something. I haven't done anything lately, but he's a cop, so he could dig stuff up if he really tried.

I'm baffled right now, though, because he's smiling.

"What?" I'm still waiting, wonder if he's finally lost it, and this is his Jack Nicholson "Here's Johnny," *The Shining* moment. I sit up taller, ready for the ax to fall, thinking I must have done something *really* bad.

His grin widens. "You've been getting some calls from a Jacksonville number?"

"I don't know." I dig through my blankets for my phone that I tossed in here somewhere. I've been getting tons of texts, still none from Nora. There are also a few missed calls. "Yeah." I hand him the phone. "I don't know anyone in Jacksonville."

He slaps my shoulder. "Well start picking up! I just got a call from one of the North Florida lacrosse coaches. He's been trying to get in touch with you!"

"What? Why?"

Dad is hopping—legit hopping—up and down so hard he can't speak.

I'm not getting any of this. Must be the drugs. "What? Dad? What did he say?"

"He said he wants to talk to you. He wants to talk about next year." Dad's trying to catch his breath, which makes him sorta sound like a really excited Darth Vader. "They need an attackman on the team. They want you!"

I shake my head and try to understand. "No. That's impossible. I'm injured."

Dad won't stop hopping. "He doesn't care. He had a scout at the Lake Mary game, and he's seen films. He saw you play after you recovered last time. He knows you can come back. He's willing to put you on the roster. I told him the doc said you should be good to go by the time the preseason starts. He's interested, E, he's interested! WHOOOOP!"

My Dad, most low-key guy on earth, is screaming like a middle school cheerleader. Mom comes running, Ari on her heels. "What's wrong? What is it?" Her voice is high-pitched and panicked.

"Nothing!" Dad says, still jumping. "Your son! Is going! To the University of North Florida! The coach wants him!"

"Wait," I say. Even though Mr. Chaffee told me to go

ahead and get my hopes up, my hopes have spent the last week or so dashed to the ground. I think it's smart to proceed with caution. "How could this happen? What about my grades?"

Dad keeps his feet on the ground, still smiling. "He said as long as you don't blow this last semester—which you *won't*—and retake the ACT—which you *will*—and improve your score, you can get in. He even said there might be some scholarship money if we jump right on it."

"*No!*" Mom yells. Now she's jumping up with him and also crying. Ari has his hands on his ears. Loud noises freak him out, but I can tell he knows this is a happy thing.

I can't jump up and down. Plus I'm in shock. I think back to my hallway conversation with Mr. Chaffee, him telling me about his friend at UNF. Did he make this happen?

"Eli?" Mom stops and hits me with her worried face. "Honey, aren't you happy? Is this what you want?"

Dad doesn't give me a second to answer. "Hell yeah, this is what he wants!" He leans over me and messes up my hair.

I don't know what to say. "Yeah, I'm happy. I just…"

I am happy. Really happy. Like I want to sound a barbaric yawp happy. But I don't want to call Koviak or any of the other guys, or even Coach. My first instinct, always, good news or bad, is to tell Nora. My best friend. Used to be my best friend. Might have been more if I hadn't been such a stupid jackass.

Mom lays her hand on my cheek. "Just what? What is it, Eli?"

I just want Nora.

Too bad I've ruined that. Ruined us.

Shit.

Chapter Twenty-Seven

NORA

Not surprisingly, after its disastrous beginning, spring break, so far, is turning out to be total crap. I haven't seen Eli at all since that awful day. Mom told me the surgery went well. I acted interested, even though I wasn't. She asked me what she should bring him. I almost told her pie from the Mermaid, then I caved and told her I'd get him something. I drove to the Tick Tock and bought the pie, but made her deliver it.

When I was there, I glanced at our booth. Not *our* booth. The booth we happened to sit in together.

I'm just saying, Nora. Have you ever wondered, if you tried again, now, to kiss me, if it would be different?

That's what he said to me that night. I should have seen right through him, should have seen that he was trying to charm me with pie and those glasses and his blue eyes and that dimple.

He might think that the pie Mom dropped off was a sign that I forgive him, but I don't.

Why should I? He doesn't care about me at all. I was going to give him a second chance and he humiliated me.

Then there was that visit with Gigi—her words have echoed through my brain all week long, and not just because they totally smashed my hypothesis into tiny bits. It was the *don't let it pass you by.* Meaning love. As far as me and Eli, it's too late. It has to be after the things he said to me, and the things he did. He "made" me fall for him? So he could teach me a lesson?

No. Just. No.

It's Wednesday, and so far all I've really done is spend part of each day watching Netflix, and the rest of it in prep for the Science Olympiad state competition, which happens in a few weeks. I qualified for the Disease Detective team and also Ecology sections, which is a big deal. Abby's going, too, if I can keep her from falling off the senior year deep end— which she seems determined to do.

When we study, all she talks about is prom and senior picnic and senior awards night, and she's still pressing me to go to the senior bonfire at the beach tomorrow night, mostly because she told her parents she'd be with me. At least if we go together, she won't be telling a complete lie. That's her reasoning.

I try to explain why I don't want to go. Without going into the details, I tell her that Eli and I had a terrible fight. That we're not friends anymore and I don't want to see him.

She wasn't having it. "Only you would break up with someone before you actually date him!" she said. "He's not even going to be there, probably, so what do you care? There will be plenty of other hot guys—get you some nice rebound action."

My mother, in a move copied by no reasonable mother *anywhere*, also encourages me to go to the bonfire.

At breakfast, she lifts her cup of coffee and grins when I tell her about it and how I don't want to go. I've never seen a smile that big on her face. "Oh, you're going."

She's been so pushy lately.

"Mom. No. I really don't want to, and I have to study." I take a bite of the scrambled eggs she made me on the hot plate. The kitchen is more of a mess since she decided to make good on her promise to start fixing things. A handyman has been here all week. The oven is finally gone, as is the drywall that was scorched behind it.

"Nora. No way. You've been studying all week. What are you, a hermit, or an eighteen-year-old woman?" She takes another swig of coffee. "Come on, Nora. YOLO!"

I spurt out a laugh. "YOLO? Oh God, Mom."

"What? Is YOLO not cool anymore?"

My stomach twists, remembering when Eli used it to talk me into the beach. "Only if you're being ironic, and you're under twenty."

She gets up for more coffee. "Oh, so sorry. Didn't realize I was so off-trend—and old. You *are* going to that bonfire, though. I insist on it."

I sip my own coffee. "You know, most mothers wouldn't send their children to a party where there will likely be illegal substances and probably clandestine sexual activity."

She walks to me and kisses the top of my head. "And most mothers don't have children who know the meaning of the word clandestine. I think I'll take my chances. It's not like I'll be around to tell you what to do when you go to Emory."

"*If* I go to Emory."

"You *will* go to Emory."

She leaves to study, and I sit in the kitchen, alone, in the quiet and construction dust. I'm going to college. That's something I try not to think about often, mostly because I don't know what's going to happen yet. It's exciting, yeah, maybe a little terrifying, too? Not much has changed since Mom and I showed up to live with Gigi all those years ago. But this year, with her moving to the center, has been hard. No matter what she says, I worry about Mom. Like me, she's not a big fan of change. I worry about myself, too.

Like what am I going to do with no more Eli? He's been a constant in my life for the last decade. I can't imagine my life without him. How will I adapt?

Adaptation means survival. If animals can't keep up with changes in their environment, they become endangered. If nothing changes, eventually they become extinct. Take the Florida fairy shrimp. The species lived in a pond south of Gainesville. Some developer bought the land, filled in the pond, and boom. Those shrimp haven't been found anywhere since.

I could be the next Florida fairy shrimp. If I fear change, if I don't try new things, if I stubbornly stick with my hypothesis and refuse to change, I could end up alone, homeless, looking for my pond, eventually dead.

Marie zooms into the kitchen, skids to a stop on the wood floor, looks up at me, and meows loudly like she's trying to send me a message. At least I'll have my cat.

Holy cow, I'm going to be a cat lady.

I push away my plate and pick her up. "There are worse things to be."

Later that night, lounging in bed with the cat sound asleep next to me, I pause the bad Netflix movie I'm watching and check my email.

When I open my inbox, I sit up so fast that Marie rockets

across the room and out the door.

The whole world comes to a screeching halt. There's a message from Emory.

Re: Scholarship

Oh God. My stomach rumbles. My heart races. My palms erupt in sweat. I wipe them off as my finger hovers over the touchpad.

I can't.

I'm scared.

I get out of bed and pace around the room. Mom's on a girls' night out with her teeth-scraping classmates. If she were here, I'd make her read it for me.

Only she's not here, and it's there—the answer I've been waiting for-slash-dreading. Whether I read it or not, my future is literally in front of me, in my inbox. Like a present, waiting to be opened.

It could be a lot of money. It could be a big pile of nothing.

I don't know what to do. I march back and forth some more and stare out the back window. It's dark over there. If only there was someone else to read it for me. If only I could still ask my best friend. Nope. No. There's no one else.

Air. I need it. In through my nose, out through my mouth. I do it again. Then I sit down on my bed and click open the email.

Okay.

It starts with *CONGRATULATIONS!*

Which is better than *SORRY.*

I scan the letter so fast that I'm sure I'm skipping over important things. There's a dollar amount, in bold.

That's what they are giving me? For four years? As long as I keep a blah, blah, GPA, blah, blah.

I do the math in my head and disappointment falls on me like an avalanche. It's not enough. Almost enough, but Emory is private and expensive and...I'm APPROVED

FOR WORK STUDY.

Work study should make up for the rest of the cost of tuition, and room and board.

I'm shaking, not believing what I'm reading. Holy cow. I can go to Emory.

I flop backward onto the mattress. I am dead.

Marie zips back into room, hops onto my bed to check that I am in fact, not dead. I cradle her in my hands and think of the weird randomness of life. I almost killed her in the road because I wanted to learn how to drive, but really because I needed to get over Eli so I could move on with my hypothesis, unhindered by the weight of my massive crush on him.

Which, let's face it, was more than a crush. I know this because of the gaping hole that he's left behind. It wasn't just the glasses or his body or his blue eyes or the dimple. It was the whole Eli.

Even if he did turn out to be a liar, a jerk, and a Neanderthal, I was in love with him, I know that now. I think I have been for a long time, and now it's time to let go. Emory will help with that.

I kiss the top of Marie's head. "It's going to happen, girl," I say into the quiet of my room. "I'm going to be a scientist."

I hear a rumble out on the driveway that makes me sit up straight. I try to fight it—and fail. I have to know what's happening. I jump out of bed and run to the bathroom, up onto my toes, to peek out the window.

I am hopeless.

It's him, it's Eli, getting out of an old car. Not Michael Jordan. His dad gets out of the passenger side and comes around to help him with his crutches.

I watch them make their way to the back door together, while his mom and Ari come outside, too, walking to the car, circling it.

He got a new car. Michael Jordan is gone?

More changes that I'm not a part of—that I *can't* be a part of anymore—just like I can't text him about Emory. Even if it goes against every instinct I have. I go back into my room where Marie Curie is cleaning herself.

Yep, it's just me and my cat.

Abby sends a text.

We're on for tomorrow, yeah?

I fall back into bed, a part of me so happy, the other part missing him so bad. At least if I go to the stupid bonfire, I won't be sitting around here thinking about Emory, or mourning my friendship, or whatever it was, with Eli. Unless he's there, too. Abby seems to think he won't be, and he did just have surgery, so it's probably safe.

Still. I can't hide from him forever. I *am* the girl next door.

Be here at 6, I text Abby.

Ooooh yes, she answers, along with a smiling emoji, a wink emoji, and two beer glasses, clinking together.

God, what am I getting myself into? I bite my bottom lip and reread the Emory email. *Be happy,* I tell myself. *Just be happy.* I let myself imagine something as amazing as work study, where I get to make money maybe conducting experiments. That's cool.

Didn't think you'd go for it, Abby texts again. *Glad you changed ur mind*

YOLO, I text her along with a rolling eyes emoji, and I remind myself that change can be good, and change can be terrifying, and I have zero control over anything, even if I'd like to believe otherwise. The only thing I know for sure is that change is going to happen, no matter what I do.

It's called chaos theory. Look it up.

Chapter Twenty-Eight

ELI

It's Wednesday night, and so far, spring break has been a steady mix of good and bad. Even the good stings, though, because I can't share it with her.

The bad: first, rehab hurts like a sonofabitch. Second, Nora and I have totally fallen off each other's radars. I didn't prove shit about her theory. I only proved that I'm an idiot, and now she hates me. These last few days, I've been wondering if there's anything I can do to salvage this wreck, and if there is, do I even have the balls to do it?

But the good? After I got the news about North Florida (go Ospreys!) Dad was suddenly feeling very generous. We went down to his mechanic, and the guy gave us a thousand bucks for Michael Jordan. It was a sad good-bye. I took off a strip of his duct tape and tucked it into my pocket so I'd remember him forever.

Then we went to another friend of Dad's who said he'd sell us his mother-in-law's old Civic for three thousand bucks, which my cheap-ass father actually paid him. The car's only fifteen years old, with only a hundred thousand miles. It's this dull-beige color and smells like old lady. It's got some personality in it, somewhere, though, and I'll bring it out eventually.

Good and bad, like I said.

I'm lying on the sofa downstairs, my face in a slice of pie, this time lemon meringue. Yeah, I made it. It's not like it's hard, although the bottom crust on this one got a little soggy. Didn't blind bake it long enough. If you don't know what blind baking is, don't bother ever making a pie.

Ari and I are watching *SpongeBob* again. Little yellow dude is starting to show up in my dreams, which is probably better than my neighbor popping up in them.

All of a sudden, a bunch of headlights shine on our living room wall. I hear car doors opening and closing and music playing in the distance.

There's banging on the front door, Mom runs in to answer. Ari jumps up, puts his hands on his ears. "What in the name of all that is good—" she shouts and there's Koviak, fresh from the game. Somewhere behind him I hear the unmistakable sound of "You Can Call Me Al."

I'm not in the mood for visitors, sitting like I am in my boxers with my slice of half-eaten pie, but what can I say? It's my team.

Koviak, one of the only people who knows about UNF, comes in and drops a sheet cake on the coffee table in front of me. It says, in totally not professional frosting letters: *WTF is an Osprey?*

That's pretty funny. The guys are loud, though, and I'm worried about Ari.

"I'll get some plates," Mom says, and takes Ari with her into the kitchen.

The guys take turns congratulating me, and there's Tex,

in my living room, saying good luck at UNF. I want to hate the dude, but I can't seem to make myself do it, even if he does end up with her. It's not his fault. Actually, if they end up together, it's probably mine. Mom serves up the cake and passes around plastic forks. We won the game, the guys tell me. This is the third win in a row, and it's about damn time. They're in a good mood and celebrating, and they obviously heard about my spot on the UNF team. They don't know that it's not a done deal, and that I gotta somehow pull up my grades. I plan on trying hard. Hope that will be enough.

When they've all had their fill, they start filtering out, all of them except for Koviak. Mom and Ari go out to walk the dog. Dad's at work.

Koviak reaches into his letter jacket pockets and pulls out two cans of beer.

I can only stare blankly. He's a madman. "Seriously?"

He flips them open and glances toward the kitchen door. "Better drink 'em fast before the chief gets home."

"Or my mom comes back."

"I didn't bring her one." He smirks and lifts the can. "Cheers, brah."

I snort and take the beer. "You're such a dumbass," I say, and since I'm off the painkillers and I did just have my knee cut open, I chug the whole thing in about ten seconds. He does the same. Burps come out of us that remind me of Mr. Chaffee's barbarous yawps. I don't share that with Koviak. This isn't Walt Whitman World, this is Neanderthal time.

He takes the empty cans and sticks them back into the pockets they came from.

I lay my head back on the sofa cushion. "You're nuts."

Cue his wicked grin. "Had to do it. It's a party, dude." He sits back and puts his feet on the coffee table. "So, how's it going KNEE-li?"

If that's my new nickname I'm quitting school. "That's

hilarious, asshole." I lift my leg up to the sofa cushion again, like I was doing before we were invaded.

"Yeah. I am. Hey, I heard you got into some sort of fight with your girl next door."

This town is too damn small. I glare at him. "Jesus, give me a break. Where'd you hear that?"

He throws his arms along the back of the love seat. Cocky asshole. "I have my sources."

The last thing I want is to talk about Nora. "Sources?"

"Yeah."

I sneer. "What, like Veronica?"

He shakes his head. "Come on. This is someone reliable. Someone on the inside."

I don't know if it's the chugged beer or what, but I feel nauseated. I snatch up the remote, about to press play again. "What do you care, anyway?" He can leave anytime. I'm more than ready to sink back into the stress-free world of Bikini Bottom. "You and your *source* should mind your own business."

Kov laughs. "Oh, what? Now that you're going to a *real* college, you think you're above the rest of us? I see how it's gonna play out."

I press play and turn up the volume. "Dude, shut up, you're going to Tampa." Tampa is like the number one Division II team in the country.

"True. But you know, Highlanders lax, first, always. My boyz." He beats his chest twice.

I chuckle. He's such a dick. "Whatever you say, Kov."

"Look," he says. "I know you think you got this 'love' thing figured out." He leans forward, elbows on his knees and touches his fingertips together, like a shrink.

"You're wrong," he continues. "You and her, dude, I mean, come on. That's something that should happen. Everyone knows it."

I wish I could tell him what I did to her. Maybe then he'd stop trying to get us together. "Everyone, who? Nothing's going to happen. Less than zero chance. Not ever."

"Because of this alleged fight?"

I don't know why he's not letting this go, but I'm getting annoyed. "No. Because she hates me." I turn up the volume some more and adjust my leg, trying to get comfortable, which I don't think is gonna happen if we keep talking about Nora.

Koviak sits up. "Dude, what if I told you she doesn't hate you?"

"I'd say you're full of shit."

He lifts a hand to his heart. "No, I swear. My source confirms. Nora doesn't hate you. You still have a chance."

Apparently, he's not ever going to stop talking. "Abby? Is that who you're talking about?"

He says nothing but tips his head in confirmation.

"I didn't know you even knew her," I say.

Kov doesn't respond right away, which is not like him. He's actually thinking about this girl. "Only in a matchmaking capacity. It's a goodwill effort. Although she *is* sexy as hell."

"Hey, Koviak, a word of advice about females like them, Abby and Nora? They hear you talk like that and they'll rip your nuts off."

"Dude," he says. "Don't worry about me. All I know is that Nora will be at the bonfire tomorrow night, and you will be, too."

"No. I won't." I watch the TV, hoping he'll get the hint. "No way. We're not a thing. We can't be. I'm not going."

There. Argument over. Shut the hell up.

He half shrugs. "Then you're an idiot."

"Oh yeah? Why am I an idiot, Kov?"

"You really want to know?"

That shit-eating grin of his is pissing me off. "Yeah, please enlighten me with your wisdom, oh Jedi of love."

He leans forward, in my face. I've only ever seen him look this serious when we're on the field.

"Dude. Life...is like lacrosse."

It's hard to keep a straight face. "Really?" I chuckle. "Didn't realize that."

"Then it's about time you did, son," he says. "In lacrosse, you defend your team, you play hard, you make some goals, miss some goals, but in the end, no matter what you do, how hard you play, how much you give, it all ends in sixty damn minutes. When the buzzer goes off, it's game over."

"Wow." I raise an eyebrow. "What the hell have you been smoking?"

He leans back on the cushion. "I'm just saying. Come to the bonfire. Don't let the buzzer go off, dude. You won't always have another chance to score."

I can't listen to this. "You're such a dick," I say.

He lifts a finger. "Ah, but a wise dick I am," he says, trying to sound like Yoda.

I don't respond, I turn all my attention to *SpongeBob*. Or I try. Kov's not right, I don't have a chance. She'd never give me a chance.

He kicks his feet onto the coffee table. "Dude, it's the iron butt episode! I fucking love this one."

Ari comes back in after a while and Koviak sticks around to watch a bunch of episodes with us. I barely see the screen. I'm thinking about Nora the whole time.

Eventually he leaves and I make my way upstairs to go to bed, stopping at the landing window that looks out to her house. It's dark over there, and my mind goes to places that it shouldn't. Up the stairs in her house, into her room, where I haven't been for years. That big, soft bed. I imagine her inviting me up there—I wouldn't go uninvited, because she'd kick my ass if I did—but in this scenario, she'd ask, and I'd lay her back onto that bed, surrounded by fluffy pillows and posters of Albert Einstein and the periodic table. Then I'd kiss her. Hard. And there'd be lightning and thunder and torrential rain. Hell, together we'd make a whole category five hurricane. Catastrophic damage would occur in that bedroom.

Now it's never gonna happen. I blew it. Didn't I?

As I hobble up the rest of the stairs, somewhere in those same dark corners of my brain, I hear a timer counting down. I'm pretty sure the game is over. Maybe it should be. Or maybe the clock's in overtime, and it's worth one last Hail Mary play before the buzzer goes off and she's gone forever.

Chapter Twenty-Nine

NORA

The next morning, Mom pops her head into my room.

"What's up, buttercup?" she asks in her dorky Mom way. I don't hold it against her, though, because she looks wrecked. It's midterms in dental hygiene school this week and she's been at study groups late, trying to get this certificate that will allow her to get paid to clean people's teeth.

"Nothing," I say. Not entirely true, of course I'm not about to share with her that I had dreams last night that should disturb me about a certain boy next door. At this point I wonder if it'll ever be possible to completely exorcise Eli from my life, from my brain, from my heart.

Then I remember, like a light flickering on. I hold back a smile. "Oh yeah," I say. "I got an email from Emory."

Instantly, her forehead crinkles up in worry. "Oh? And?"

I have to force my mouth not to turn upward. "I did get some scholarship money."

"What?" She's still worried. "Oh my God. How much?"

She presses her hands together, holds them up to her mouth, like she's praying. "Oh my God, tell me!"

That's it. I can't hold it in. "Most of it, Mom, and I qualified for work study, which they say should cover the rest. For four years."

Then my mother screams. "Ohmygod! You did it! You did it!" She throws herself on my still-horizontal self and grabs me in a hug. "You did it! You did it!"

I start laughing and can't stop. Mom has always been my biggest cheerleader, and right now she's acting like I won a gold medal in the Olympics or something, which it feels like I sort of did.

She climbs onto my bed, sits cross-legged and starts to cry.

I sit up, swipe a tear off her cheek, and tug on her pajama sleeve. "Mom? What's wrong?"

She sniffs and rubs at her eyes. "Nothing. Nothing's wrong! I'm just so proud of you, and amazed by you. You're amazing." She sniffs again. "You know that?"

"I'm just a good student, Ma, not amazing."

I lie back, head on my pillow and she flops down at my side. She wraps her arm around me and pulls me to her, then kisses the top of my head. I feel like a tiny girl again, and I don't mind at all.

"You *are* a good student, but you're so much more, honey. God, I'm so happy for you. You have the world at your feet, and that's all I've ever wanted for you—the adventure is about to begin!"

She squeezes me tighter and cries some more, and I'm surprised to find myself with tears in my eyes, too. This time I don't feel like they are a waste of time. This time, they feel good.

Suddenly, she sits up. "Hey, let's celebrate, let's go get breakfast!" As she shimmies off my bed, her happy face turns back to me. "We can ask Eli, too!"

My smile is gone. "Eli?"

"Yeah, I mean, both of you—going away to school! I can't believe it!" She must see in my face that I don't know what she's talking about, because she frowns. "Wait. You don't know? Are you still in a fight?"

My nonanswer is her answer.

I swallow hard. "Eli is going away to school?"

She edges closer. "Yes? Oh, honey, I assumed you knew. He got a call from the UNF coach. They want him to play lacrosse."

It feels like I just got punched in the stomach. I sit up, my back to Mom, so I can pull myself together. "Oh. Jacksonville?"

"I'm sorry. I assumed you two had patched everything up."

"No." I bite my bottom lip. "But good for him!"

My voice is high, and barely recognizable. I'm trying to take the high road for my mother's sake, and be the bigger person. Except I don't feel bigger. All I feel is my heart break a little bit more, and here I'd thought it was already shattered into microscopic pieces.

To make matters worse, after a slice of subpar blueberry pie at the Mermaid for breakfast, we go to see Gigi, who doesn't remember us at all.

I almost cancel with Abby. I don't feel like going to the bonfire. I don't want to see all those people. I don't want to hear the sneers of the girls who think I'm cold. I don't want to hear them say that Eli is hot. I don't want to see his teammates. I don't want to go.

Oh hell no, Abby texts me when I let her know my

feelings.

At six sharp, she pulls up to the house, ready to go, not taking no for an answer.

One thing that's good—I'm glad that Abby and I have started to hang out again, even if she *is* only using me as a cover for being perpetually grounded. I've missed her. We have a lot in common, and when I tell her I got the scholarship, her reaction is pretty much just like Mom's.

"We are so getting you drunk tonight," she says once we're inside my car.

My body stiffens and I wonder if she's serious. I'm not going down the vodka-orange juice road with her again. "You don't even want to drive with me when I'm sober," I joke, trying to calm myself. Even though I'm legal now, there's still a wave of anxiety that sweeps over me every time I buckle up. I can still hear that poor woman scream, and I can also still imagine Eli beside me, trying to calm me down.

None of that is good.

At least his new piece of crap car—is that duct tape on the bumper?—is still in the driveway. Which means he isn't going to the bonfire. Good. That's exactly what I hoped for.

I inhale and exhale, channeling my inner capable driver, and we're off, my mother waving from the driveway, tears still rolling down her face.

The bonfire is at someone's grandparents' beach house. It's a long way off the main road, it's dark, and I have no idea where I'm going, so by the time we get there, I'm frazzled.

I park and Abby swats my arm. "That was some first-class driving, girlfriend," she says.

I guess she's right, but there's still a giant ball of anxiety in my stomach. It's not just about the driving, it's everything.

Especially Eli. I've never done one of these things without him around.

Abby opens her door. "Come on, Nora, let's own this bonfire."

I'm not owning anything, but I follow her anyway.

We walk a few blocks to the house. It's obvious that retirees live here. There are vases full of fake plastic flowers and plastic on all the furniture, which actually makes it perfect for a high school party. Go ahead, puke on the chair, it'll wipe right up!

Almost immediately, Abby gets sucked into a group of girls that includes Veronica. When I think of her nasty comments at O'Dell's, I make a beeline to the sliding glass doors at the back of the house.

It's cooler tonight, the heat wave of the last few weeks finally lifting. I go out onto the deck, past a bunch of patio furniture where there are several couples making out. It's impossible to tell who they are, and it would be weird to look too closely, so I pass through them quickly.

Out at the keg a few of the lax guys are filling their cups. "Hey, Nora," one of them says. It's Koviak, who hands me a cup. "Here, just poured this for ya."

Even though I'm the designated driver, Koviak is a friend of Eli's, and he's being nice to me. I decide to keep my mouth shut and take the beer.

"Thank you," I say.

He starts to pump another cup. "So, did you come with your boy?"

I might have spoken too soon. "My *boy*?"

"Yeah. Eli?"

I raise my cup, take a tiny sip, and cringe. God, beer is so gross. "Not my boy. And no, he's not with me."

Truer words were never spoken.

I turn away. The beach is in front of me, a wide stretch

of it, filled with people I've known since I was nine years old. Friends, acquaintances, strangers, maybe a nemesis or two.

But no Eli, who at the moment feels like a mix of all those things.

Out on the sand, there's a group trying to start the bonfire, and I see Caleb in silhouette. I guess I should probably go ahead and kiss him, except my hypothesis is in pieces, and the truth is, I still don't want to.

I walk down the wooden deck stairs, take off my shoes, and let my feet sink in as I gaze at the sky. I'm pretty sure no one else here knows that the moon is in a waning gibbous phase, just after a full moon. That's why it's so bright, lighting up the sky and reflecting off the mirror smooth Gulf water.

It makes me think of the picnic, and being with Eli out in the water. Our first near-kiss since the actual kiss when we were kids. I shiver thinking how badly I wanted it to happen. I know this much—when I go to college in the fall, I have to toughen up. I can't be so naive. I can't let myself fall so hard. Even if my hypothesis has changed, I can still be rational and keep my head.

What other choice do I have if I don't want a life filled with this kind of heartbreak?

I have to say, it totally sucks.

Chapter Thirty

ELI

I have a new plan.

My Hail Mary.

I went to the store today, bought some blueberries, and worked on a pie. The first one was crap. The second one's crust burned. I guess the third one was okay. I'm not making a fourth damn pie, not even if it's my last chance with Nora.

Ari's been bugging me all night because he wants to eat it. The only thing that's holding him back from taking a slice? His love for all things Nora.

We have that much in common—we both love her. When I told him it was for her, he smiled really big like he knew what I was thinking. He isn't usually keyed in to other people's emotions, so I might be wrong, but my brother surprises me all the time.

My plan is whack, and I'm fucking terrified. I'm taking it over there when she gets home from the bonfire. I'm doing it—telling her what I should have told her the other day. *Yes,*

I should have kissed you. Yes, I want a second chance. Maybe I'll get one.

Or at least maybe I can convince her to be my friend again, even though I know that won't be enough. I want more and I have to tell her so. That's why I'm nervous as hell.

I'm pacing around the house like a caged animal on crutches when a text comes through from Koviak.

Dude, you better come and get ur girl

There goes my pulse again, skyrocketing. What's that mean? I don't text him back. Instead I check my phone. There are plenty of posts about the party. It's probably gonna get busted—these things usually are—and what if Nora gets caught? Who will driver her home if she's been drinking? I know she drove, I saw her and Abby leave. What if Tex takes her home? Or anyone else? Anyone but me?

I stalk across my bedroom, at least, as much as I can with this knee. I have such a clear picture of her in my mind, tears falling down her face while I yelled at her.

I'm such a dick!

That's it. I can't stay here anymore. I fly downstairs, somehow without killing myself, into the kitchen, where Ari's sitting doing the *New York Times* crossword puzzle. Kid's so smart, he finishes it every day.

"Ari?"

"Eli."

Mom and Dad went out to a movie, and I can't leave him alone at home.

Everything in me wants to run out of here, but I need to keep my brother calm. I've got my eyes on the pie, which he still hasn't touched. "You wanna go for a drive?"

He puts down his pen. He does the damn *New York Times* crossword *in pen*.

"To where?"

I steel myself for this last play, for my last chance to win the heart of the girl next door.

"I gotta deliver a pie."

Chapter Thirty-One

NORA

I've walked down to the neighboring beach house, out of sight of the group of kids around the bonfire, which is blazing now. Lying on my back on the dry sand, legs stretched out in front of me, I stare at that amazing moon. I think of physics, and gravity, and the laws that govern the world. I'm trying to not think about Eli, but inevitably it all comes back to him.

"Hey, Nora." I hear a familiar voice from behind. "Want some company?"

It's Caleb. He found me. He sits down, and I can't say I don't welcome the distraction. Plus if we're actually going to be friends, I suppose there's no time like the present.

"You wanna come hang out by the fire?" He takes a sip from the plastic cup he's holding and looks down at me. The drink that Koviak gave me is beside me in the sand, untouched except for that first sip. I want to keep my wits about me and not do anything I'll regret.

I sigh. "Nah, I'm good."

"You okay?"

I shiver and sit up, hugging my knees to my chest. The temperature is dropping and without a word, Caleb takes off his hoodie, puts it on my back, and props it up on my shoulders, like the stand-up guy that he is.

"Thank you." I wonder if I made a mistake, not kissing him, and then remind myself that I didn't want to, and I still don't want to. I still want…

A voice carries across the sand.

"Nora Reid?"

I jerk my head backward in disbelief, and push myself up to standing.

"Ari?"

There he is, trundling down the sand.

I gasp. Behind him is Eli, trying to navigate the beach on crutches in the moonlight.

God, he's perfect.

No. He's not. He's mean and he broke my heart. I focus on Ari. "What are you doing here?"

He hits me with the bottomless dimple, just like his brother. "I brought you a pie." He holds out his hands, which are, like he said, holding a foil-covered, pie-shaped object. "Eli made it," he says. "It's for you. Can I have some?"

I look at Eli. He's stopped about ten yards away.

I glance at Caleb, feeling the weight of his jacket on my shoulders.

"Hey, Eli," Caleb says, slow, with the drawl.

Eli nods at him. "Caleb."

He turns back to me. "I'm just gonna go back over to the fire."

I start to take off his hoodie.

"Nah." He stops me. "You keep it, it's cold out here." He sticks his hands in his front pockets, looks to Eli again, then walks away.

I feel a weight lift off me. Eli brought me a pie. But what does that mean?

Eli takes an awkward step backward. "No," he says. "He doesn't have to leave. We should go. Come on, Ari," he says. He turns around, then walks away—or tries to.

Wait, that's it?

A wave of anger hits me hard, like a riptide pulling me under. "So, what, you just came to drop off a pie and leave?" I yell at him. Everyone at the bonfire hears me and turns toward us, and I don't care. "What do you want, Eli?"

"I…" He maneuvers back around and tries to move closer, but his crutches are sinking. He's going to kill himself out in this sand. "Nothing. I just wanted to bring you something."

"Yeah, a pie. Got it, thanks!"

"Yes," he says, louder now. "A pie."

I'm shaking, inside and out. "Why?"

For a long second he stands there, like he's thinking about his words. "Because—PFE—right? And I want to be your friend again."

"Friend?" The word hurts for a reason that makes no sense. Standing there, I realize I can't go back to being his friend. I want more than that, and that's not going to happen. "No. Friends don't make friends 'fall for them' to prove them wrong. You really think I'm that easy?"

The corners of his mouth curve up slowly. "No, Nora. I don't think you're easy. I think you're hard. You're *so* hard. A total pain in the ass."

Those words burn in me. I want to scream. "Oh, that's just great!"

His hard eyes soften. "Yeah, and also, you're the most amazing person I know," he yells, trying to make his way closer to me.

Everyone is watching us. God, we'll probably end up on YouTube.

"No!" I hold up my hand. "No, you don't. You're a liar. Go away with your evil pie of *lies*."

Ari still has it, standing off to the side, watching us like a tennis match. I check to make sure he's not getting upset. Meanwhile, his brother is almost in front of me.

He looks at me and grins. That stupid grin with the ridiculous dimple.

I'm not falling for it this time. "You think this is a joke? Just like these last few weeks? A big joke! Why? Why did you do it? Do you really hate me that much?"

My voice is shaking. *I* am shaking.

He's oddly still. "No. I didn't do it because I hate you." His voice is solid and sure.

I don't want to hear his excuses. I turn around and walk away, down the beach. I can't listen to how he planned to hurt me. It'll probably kill me.

"I did it because I love you!" he yells.

Chapter Thirty-Two

ELI

Yeah. I just said that. Out loud. It felt good.

"I love you," I say it again like I'm trying the words on for size, and they fit. I need to be closer to her. I'm trying, but these goddamn crutches are not cooperating. I want to chuck them across the beach and walk over to her like a regular guy with two good knees. That's not in the cards, though, so I just stand there looking like an idiot.

She laughs—it isn't a good laugh. Great. I finally have the guts to say it, and she doesn't believe me. I force the damn crutches to go and stab my way through the sand toward her. *Get ready, Costas. Prepare for total rejection.*

"Go ahead, Ari," she says to my brother, who is still holding the pie. "You can have the whole thing."

Her hands make fists and she plants them on her hips. Badass Nora Reid. Can't tell her what to do or think.

She's done talking, and my heart's gonna fail it's pumping so hard right now. I'm probably gonna break my knee for good trying to cross this beach. It takes forever, but finally, I get to her.

"You are a liar," she says.

"I'm not lying." It's weird. I'm in sand, on crutches, in front of a girl in another dude's hoodie. This doesn't look good for me at all, I know that. So why have I never felt more confident in my life that I'm at the right place, at the right time? This is chance, and I'm lined up for the shot.

I take a deep breath. "I love you."

She's worried—biting the lip *and* scrunching her nose. "Fuck you," she says.

Wow. I smile. "Nora. You hate that word."

She crosses her arms. "So? Sometimes it's the only word that works."

Her hair blows in the breeze. Her wild hair. The brown eyes. Damn. They're shining in the light of this giant-ass moon.

"You hurt me, Eli."

I move closer, and she doesn't back away. A good sign? "Yeah. I know. I was scared." I have to tell her the truth—my only chance to make the goal is to give it 100 percent.

She gives me that *I don't believe you* scowl. "Scared of what?"

I take a minute. I need to make sure the words are right. "The usual, I guess," I finally say. "What if we suck? What if I lose you? All that bullshit."

Her chin drops to her chest. "You *made* me fall in love with you." Her voice breaks.

I move closer, forcing the crutches to do what I want. I'll crawl to her if I have to. This is a story she needs to hear.

"Yeah, I admit, I tried," I say. "But to be honest, you made me fall in love with you first."

Her eyes lift, they're doing the twinkling thing. God, she's beautiful. "How do you know that?"

I feel the entire student body of EHS watching us. Hail Mary, baby.

"That first day, on Gigi's porch," I say. "Your hair that day looked exactly like it does now. Wild. Your teeth, all purple. Your giant eyes. You know your eyes are giant? Those things totally sucked me in. From that very first day—I loved you."

Her gaze flutters to the sand, then jerks back up. "That's not true."

She still isn't buying it, so I keep moving closer; I can't stop now. She's so stubborn, and sometimes to convince Nora Reid of something, you gotta get in her face.

"I wasn't planning to ever tell you that," I say. "Especially after that kiss. You wouldn't have listened." I drop one crutch, lean my weight on my good leg, hop the last little bit, and close the distance between us.

I use my free hand to reach out to her, now I'm close enough to smell her hair. I can't describe that smell. It just smells like Nora, and it slays me. I move my arm around her waist, aware that she could take me down at any second.

She doesn't. I reach her back, pull her close.

She just stands there, looking confused. I wonder if she's about to topple me. I don't care if she does.

"It wasn't real," she whispers. "The beach, the drives, the garage. You didn't mean any of it." Then she lifts her hand and touches the collar of my T-shirt. Her fingers brush my neck. I'm gonna die now.

Everything about her is attacking my senses, her smell, the sight of her, the sound of her breathing, the feel of her in my arms. "No," I say. "I meant *all* of it. I thought you were trying to get your license so that you could go to Emory and start testing your hypothesis there. I thought you might find someone else. Someone who wasn't me."

She presses her lips together. I notice because I'm watching them now. "I wanted to drive because I couldn't stop thinking about you. I thought maybe you were affecting my results. That's all it was. Because I hate driving. I really hate it."

I laugh low. "I would have driven you around, for free, for the rest of time. That's how much I love you."

She studies me for what feels like an hour. I can hear my heartbeat in my ears, the strange *whoosh* of blood rushing through my body. This is the moment. The ball is in the air. It might not be enough. It might crash to the earth. Game over. *Please, Nora, catch the ball.* Then she pulls away, and just when I think it's all over—my heart, my life, the world—Nora reaches into the front pocket of her jeans and yanks out her keys. "Okay." She winds up and tosses them out into the Gulf. There's a distant splash, and she faces me again.

"I'm all yours," she says.

My heart has stopped beating so I'm probably almost dead. The blood in my ears quiets.

What did she say?

"Yours?" I ask, in barely a whisper.

She nods once, puts her hands on my shoulders. "Yours."

I pull her close, then closer, and she lets me. Now... *Now* I'm as close as I want to be. Almost.

Our noses touch. "Scientifically speaking, this will never work, you know," she says.

Her lips, almost touching mine I swear are giving off an electric charge. I feel the buzz. "I don't give a damn about science. I just want to kiss you."

"Again?"

"Yeah. You up for it, Einstein?"

The corners of her mouth turn up and she scrunches her nose. "I don't know. When did you last have a Coke?"

"Funny," I say, and as I lean in toward her, her eyelids flutter shut. She's ready for the kiss. I smile and pull up short. "You know... There's a chance I've improved a little since eighth grade."

She laughs. I love that laugh.

"Yeah, but I've had more field experience."

Now *I* laugh. You have to, staring into those big brown eyes, knowing you're about to get everything you've ever wanted. Get caught up in those eyes and you're a dead man. I let go, and they pull me under. I'm a goner.

Chapter Thirty-Three

NORA

He's going to kiss me. Not just any *he*—Eli Costas is going to kiss me. For the second time.

I try to take it all in. Not like a heroine in a romance novel, heart racing and head in the clouds. I am a scientist. I notice details. Make observations.

Eli, this close, is even more handsome. He smells good, clean and soapy. His chin is clean shaven. His hair is perfectly messy, like he put some effort into it. I wonder if he predicted this happening tonight? Or did he just hope for a positive outcome?

I notice he's wearing the blue-green T-shirt that I love so much. He's got on his glasses, too, like he knew that would be the nail in the coffin.

He touches my face gently and I wait. For what?

Well, for the reaction, I guess. That's what we scientists do.

I take note of how sure he seems when he closes the space

between us, how determined he is. When our lips touch, it's like they're relieved to get this second chance. Like they've been waiting for it all these years. They know exactly what to do and where to go.

It's *easy*.

I observe that I am sinking into this kiss, that it covers me, like lowering myself into a hot bath. It's soothing and exhilarating, all at the same time.

The whole party claps and cheers for us, and finally, we pull apart. I feel drunk, though I've only had two sips of beer, and his lips are still in front of me, already calling me back.

"I guess you're going to need a ride home?" he whispers.

I suck in a breath and turn to the water, biting my lower lip. Why is he talking about driving at a time like—

I gasp. "Oh my God." I look to the vast, dark horizon where I will never, ever find my keys, and my stomach sinks a little bit. Why did I do that? Mom is going to kill me. I should dive in and look for them anyway, except Eli is holding me close, and I don't want him to stop.

"You didn't have to do that, you know," he says. "I would have driven you anyway."

I give the ocean one last pitiful glance, and then let myself settle back into his embrace. "I was trying to prove a point."

"Just like always," he says, and we kiss again. And again. I hope the agains never end. I hope I get to do this forever.

In the end, Gigi was right. Her earthquake was not my earthquake.

It was our second kiss that proved my hypothesis.

It wasn't *just* a kiss, of course. When our lips touched, it was like a law of physics that, like the pull of gravity, felt solid, strong, reliable. Bigger than me, bigger than Eli. Bigger than

both of us.
A little bit of science.
A little bit of chaos.
But mostly, magic.

Epilogue

NORA

I'm almost home. Thanksgiving is tomorrow and I can't wait.

I pass the sign off the highway, WELCOME TO EDINBURGH. HOME OF THE HIGHLANDERS, and I feel a pang of homesickness. I've missed it here. I haven't been back since I left for Atlanta in late August, which is less than I'd planned. Between work and studying and going to class, I have no time. I'm knee-deep in science and I *love* it.

Mom makes sure to FaceTime me every time she visits Gigi, who still has her good days and bad. Whether or not she remembers me, though, I know that she loves me, and somewhere in the locked-up parts of her brain, she knows exactly who I am.

I'm not going straight home. Someone is waiting for me at the Mermaid. When I pull in, I park my car next to his. I hop out so fast I almost forget to turn off the engine and when I slide into his front seat, not a word passes between us before we're kissing and I want to rip his shirt off.

Someone honks next to us. It's Mr. Stark, who owns the funeral home, waving hello.

I fix my shirt and wave back.

"Hi," I finally say to Eli and laugh. My smile is too big, I can feel it. I can't control it. It's going to eat my face.

"Hey," he says. He's wearing his glasses. Oh God. I want him so bad.

I kiss him again, I don't care about Mr. Stark or anyone else who might walk by. We kiss hard and deep and I never want to stop kissing Eli Costas.

When we finally break apart, his palm rests on my cheek, his fingers play with my hair. He breathes me in. "God, it's so good to see you."

He came up for a visit in October. He got to know my roommates and my friends, and got to see the campus. We explored Atlanta, and each other. We even got tattoos, his on his biceps, mine hidden on my hip. Pi symbols, of course, a blend of science and pie. I thought it was extremely clever.

"I wish school wasn't so far away," I say.

He takes my hand when I start to pick at some peeling plastic on his dashboard and gives me a warning look. "Don't start picking on Scottie Pippen." He named the car after one of Michael Jordan's teammates, apparently. "He's gotta last a while." He leans in again, until I feel the heat of his breath on my lips and I can't see straight. "So I can come and see you."

We have a tentative plan. Eli's going to major in business, get his degree, and then move up to Atlanta when I move on to graduate school. He's talked about someday opening his own bakery, and if I can be with him—and have pie whenever I want—that would be incredible.

Lacrosse, of course, will always be in the picture. He loves his new coach and the team. His knee is good and he has dreams of maybe making the Olympic team if that actually happens.

I moan, wishing we could be together sooner. "Four years..."

He looks at me with so much love and pushes back my hair. "Three and a half, more like."

He puts his hand on the back of my head and pulls me close until our foreheads touch. "Don't worry. No matter what, we'll be fine. We're meant to be. It's been proven, scientifically."

"It has?"

"Yeah," he says, "and by one of the world's most up-and-coming research scientists."

"Oh?"

His dimple deepens. "Yeah. You've heard of her. Super smart. Super hot?"

"Hmm." I twist up my mouth. "Not ringing any bells."

"Yes, you know her. She's totally in love with me. And I'm totally in love with her." His lips find mine again. This kiss, every kiss with Eli, takes over all my senses, all my nerves, all my muscles, all my everything.

"Oh, *that* scientist," I whisper as his lips move to my neck and the world spins on its axis, all the laws of physics and nature and love working together in perfect harmony, exactly as they should.

Acknowledgments

Many thanks to my agent, Danielle Chiotti, for your faith in me, for always cheering me on and for convincing me to take a chance on romance. Thank you to my editor, Heather Howland, who has taught me more about writing in the last year than I could have imagined. I so look forward to the next book, and the next. To the staff of Entangled Publishing from Liz Pelletier and Stacy Abrams to Heather Riccio and my publicity team, Melissa Montovani, Riki Cleveland, and Holly Bryant-Simpson, to Crystal Havens, and April Martinez for an amazing cover, to the copy-editing team including Curtis Svehlak, and everyone else who has had a hand in this book, thank you! I love working for such a dynamic and forward-thinking company run by such great people.

Thanks always to my writing friends. I hope you know who you are. Just in case: WWFC, the LODers, the YaHous, SCBWI Houston, and Illinois, Kristin Rae, the Class of 2k11, Amy Fellner Dominy, who read an early draft of this book, the authors of Empire Café, all the lovely bloggers and librarians. I am truly blessed to bask in the glow of your talent and generosity, and to call you my friends.

To friends and family who don't write, but nevertheless have to put up with me—I'm sorry, and thank you. I also hope you know who you are, but I'll mention by name my amazing husband, Michael, who cooks and cleans and works so hard, and makes me feel so loved. My beautiful, smart daughters and my favorite readers, Cate and Lily. Thanks Sam, too. To my extended family, far and near, especially my parents and siblings (both in-law and out), nieces and nephews, thank you for inspiring and encouraging me. To friends who are always there for me, your support means the world.

Thank you to Cindy, Ethan, and Evan Gant, whose lacrosse expertise was invaluable in the writing of this book. You are the greatest!

Many thanks to the educators, paras and students in the SFE SPEAK program, for teaching me a little something about the beauty and complexities of the human mind and heart.

Finally, thanks to God for all of my blessings and the talents You've entrusted to me. I get to do what I love every day, and I am forever grateful.

About the Author

Christina Mandelski loves to bring the characters in her head to life on the page. When she isn't writing, she enjoys spending time with her family, traveling and reading (preferably under an umbrella at the beach). Chris lives with her husband and two daughters in Houston. You can visit her at www. christinamandelski.com.

Discover more of Entangled Teen Crush's books…

OFFSETTING PENALTIES
a *Brinson Renegades* novel by Ally Matthews

Isabelle Oster is devastated when the only male dancer backs out of the fall production. Without a partner, she has no hope of earning a spot with a prestigious ballet company. All-state tight end Garret Mitchell will do anything to get a college football scholarship. Even taking ballet, because he gets to be up close and personal with the gorgeous Goth girl Izzy. But she needs him to perform with her, and he draws the line at getting on stage. *Especially* wearing tights.

SAVING IT
a novel by Monica Murphy

Eden and Josh have been best friends forever. So when Josh asks for Eden's help in finding him a girl to lose his virginity with, she agrees…except now all of a sudden she's thinking about having sex. With her best friend. And Josh is starting to think the perfect girl has been right by his side all along. Only problem? Now she thinks he's only after one thing…with anyone *but* her.

JUST ONE OF THE BOYS
a novel by Leah and Kate Rooper

Alice Bell has one goal: to play for the elite junior hockey team the Chicago Falcons. But when she's passed over at tryouts for being a girl, she'll do *anything* to make her dream a reality… even disguising herself as her twin brother. With her amazing skills on the ice, Alice is sure she'll fit in easily. That is, until she starts falling for one of her teammates…

11020899R00148

Printed in Germany
by Amazon Distribution
GmbH, Leipzig